The One You Fear

PAUL PILKINGTON

The One You Fear

CORONET

First published in Great Britain in 2014 by Coronet
An imprint of Hodder & Stoughton
An Hachette UK company

First published in paperback in 2014

1

A CIP catalogue record for this title is available from the British Library

ISBN 978 1 444 78486 2
Ebook ISBN 978 1 444 78485 5

Typeset by Hewer Text UK Ltd, Edinburgh
Printed and bound by Clays Ltd, St Ives plc

Hodder & Stoughton policy is to use papers that are natural, renewable
and recyclable products and made from wood grown in sustainable
forests. The logging and manufacturing processes are expected to
conform to the environmental regulations of the country of origin.

Hodder & Stoughton Ltd
338 Euston Road
London NW1 3BH

www.hodder.co.uk

For my family

Prologue

Margaret Myers held the remote control tightly in her hand and pointed it towards the sleeping television. She pressed the stand-by button and the box sprang to life, illuminating the otherwise dark lounge. She watched, transfixed and scared, as images played out in front of her. A policewoman, arms and legs pounding, was running down a rain-sodden street, giving chase to a man. She looked just like that girl – the one who had ruined it all with her wicked ways. The programme frightened Margaret. Programmes like that gave you funny ideas.

Two weeks ago the television had spoken to her.

It had told her that she should end it all.

Margaret Myers changed channel, her hand shaking like a jackhammer. The lottery draw – that was better. She didn't like the police programmes, didn't like them at all.

She remembered the times when the whole family would sit down in front of the television on a Saturday night and watch the quiz shows, their dinners on their laps – herself; her husband, Peter; and her dear Stephen. Back then everything was good.

But that was then, and this was now.

A man and woman had visited and told her that Peter had been arrested. He'd done something wrong. She couldn't remember what. They'd wanted her to come with them, to spend some time resting in that awful place they had taken her to a few weeks ago.

She hadn't been fooled by their weasel words and plastic smiles. This time she wasn't going anywhere. They thought she was stupid, or crazy, or both. But she knew what they were up to. They had taken her son and her husband, but they wouldn't take her.

The draw was starting. She leaned forward in anticipation as the arms in the selecting machine kicked up the balls, before sucking one up through the plastic tube and spitting it out down the chute.

And the first ball is . . . number twelve.

She caught her breath. Number twelve. Stephen had been born on the twelfth of December.

Again a ball was sucked up the tube.

And the second ball is . . . number twelve.

She blinked, shaking her head. It was a mistake. Someone had placed a duplicate ball in the machine. Why hadn't people noticed?

And the third ball is . . . number twelve.

'No, no, no, it's not right, it can't be.'

She jabbed at the controller, blackening the screen and sending the room back into darkness. For a few seconds she just sat there in the pitch black, breathing heavily, her hands curled into tight fists.

And then a noise – was someone at the door?

At first she didn't move, but just sat there in the darkness. Why would somebody be calling at such a late hour? Maybe it had been her imagination.

But there was a definite knock this time.

Margaret Myers rose from the sofa and moved into the corridor, edging slowly towards the front door.

'Hello. Who's there?' There was no answer. She grasped the door handle – but then she stopped herself. Maybe they had returned for her, to take her away to their place, evicting her for ever from the family home.

They thought they were so clever.

'Go away – I'm not coming with you. Leave me alone.'

Something was pushed through the letterbox. It fell onto the carpet, and she bent to pick it up.

It couldn't be . . .

She cradled the object in her hand, tears swelling in her eyes. 'It can't be.'

Then she grabbed the door and pulled it open.

'It's you,' she said, breaking into a broad smile. 'It's really you.' She threw her arms around him. 'They said you were dead, but I always knew you'd come back to me.'

One week later

Part One

I

Emma Holden woke in a sweat, her face damp against the pillow. At first she didn't know where she was, then she remembered. She was in a luxury holiday apartment a few miles outside the small Cornish seaside town of St Ives, down in the far south west of England. Dan had surprised her with the news that they were going away for a few days, from Friday until Tuesday. They'd both needed to get away from London for a while, just four weeks after the terrible events of Dan's kidnap at the hands of Peter Myers.

Unable to help herself, Emma allowed her mind once again to go over the recent, terrible events: back to the man who had been hell-bent on revenge for the death of his son, Stephen, who had stalked her years previously.

'Are you awake, Dan?'

There was no reply. She reached across the big double bed but her fiancé wasn't there – the covers had been pulled back and, raising her head off the pillow, she saw that the bedroom door was ajar. She sat up and only then remembered the nightmare.

It had been the same dream again, the third time in two weeks. Again it was her wedding. She and Dan had been standing in front of the altar, filled with excitement and love. Dan looked so handsome, in a dark blue suit with white shirt and pastel pink tie, his short, dark hair brushed down neatly. He had smiled and squeezed her hand. Then the dream had moved on, and suddenly it was Stephen Myers standing before her, his cat-green eyes dancing with delight and his expression keen. His gaunt face was acne-scarred and badly shaven, his side-parted brown hair slick with grease. He had looked older, but still had the same vacant stare and delusional smile. The priest had announced, 'You may now kiss the bride,' and he had lunged at her, thrusting his mouth towards hers as she tried to fight him off.

Each time she had woken at that moment, her body rigid with shock.

She lay in bed now, trying to rationalise the dream. Peter and Stephen Myers had featured strongly in the real-life nightmare that had begun four weeks ago, over that August bank holiday weekend. It was little wonder they were still present in her subconscious.

She still remembered with shocking clarity the call that had heralded the start of it all: her brother, Will, reporting that Dan was missing. He hadn't turned up for his own stag party, and couldn't be reached on his mobile. Rushing back to their flat, they'd found Dan gone, and his brother, Richard, almost beaten to death. The next week had been hell – not only had she been faced with the possibility that her fiancé had attacked his own brother and run out on her, but she was also being stalked.

Stephen Myers had been her immediate suspect – he had called himself her number one fan during her days on the soap, *Up My Street*. But then Emma had discovered that he had died four years previously, murdered by Stuart Harris, her ex-fiancé.

And therein had lain the explanation for Dan's disappearance.

It was because, years later, when Peter Myers had found out the truth about his son's death, he had taken his revenge on Emma and her family by kidnapping Dan. Thankfully they had rescued Dan in time, and Richard was recovering well.

And, given that Emma had only just been told the dark secret of Stephen's murder – it had been hidden from her not only by Stuart and Will, but also by her father, Edward – was it any wonder that she was having nightmares?

She got out of bed, went into the hallway and through into the main kitchen and living room. It was certainly an amazing apartment. The kitchen was full of top spec appliances, all of which were new: washing machine, dishwasher, oven and espresso maker – which, by the smell of it, had just been used.

Bright, early morning October sunlight was streaming through the patio doors at the far end. Dan was sitting outside on the small decking area, staring out to sea and over towards the town of St Ives to the west. On the table in front of him was the freshly made coffee. He didn't seem to notice Emma's approach – he was still staring into the distance as she reached him.

'Morning,' she said, taking the seat next to him, glad that there were two cups of coffee on the table.

Dan smiled at her. 'I woke up early and thought I'd try out the machine.' He gestured towards the cups.

'I'm impressed,' Emma said.

'You haven't tasted it yet.'

'Well, it *looks* great.'

'I've got to admit, it was my second attempt. The first time I burned it. It was revolting, so it went straight down the sink.'

'Then top marks for perseverance.' Emma smiled at him, taking a sip. 'Lovely.'

'It's such an amazing view,' Dan said, as they both looked out across the sea. A small fishing vessel was making its way from St Ives towards open water. It looked so fragile, bobbing up and down on the waves like a toy. Even though it was a spectacularly sunny morning with a flawless blue sky, there was a keen wind whipping up the water into white tips.

Emma stole a glance at Dan; his short, dark brown hair was messy from sleep in the way that she always found so endearing. He still didn't look himself, though. He had been injured physically during his time in captivity, but nothing too serious – mainly bruising, which had now healed. But, mentally – well, Emma wasn't sure. He hadn't opened up yet about what had happened during those days at the hands of Peter Myers. And although she was desperate to understand, so she could help, she didn't want to press him. He needed to be ready to talk.

'I'm worried about you,' she said, realising she hadn't intended to vocalise those thoughts.

Dan smiled sadly, as if he knew what she was talking about. 'I'm okay, Em. It's just going to take time to get over it all.'

Emma nodded. They were all finding it difficult. 'I think Lizzy is finding things tough.'

'Well, she was kidnapped by that man, too.' Emma's best friend, Lizzy, had been snatched off the street by Peter Myers, and taken to the same house where Dan was being held. Thankfully, they'd both been rescued unharmed – physically, if not mentally.

'You know,' Emma said, 'if you want to talk about it, if you think it would help, I'm always here for you.'

'I know.' Dan took her hand. 'Come here.'

Emma snuggled into his side as he placed a comforting arm around her. She closed her eyes, enjoying the brightness of the sun and the warmth of his body. 'I was so scared. I thought I might never see you again.'

Dan held her tighter. 'It's okay. I'm not going anywhere.'

Emma breathed him in, deeply. She loved him so much. She couldn't believe she'd ever loved Stuart Harris. Not only had he killed a man and dragged her brother into it, but he had used Dan's disappearance to appear in her life again, trying to win her back by recommending she be cast in a major film. She shivered as she thought of all the strings that had been pulled and tweaked without her knowing it; strings that had had her dancing unknowingly, uncomprehendingly, to someone else's menacing tune.

He woke early, showered then dressed, ready to go down for breakfast. He had slept well. The guest house was a bit tired around the edges, and in need of a lick of paint, but the bed was comfy and he had been tired from his journey. It had been a long drive.

He admired himself in the full-length mirror, flattening down his hair and straightening his brown jacket. He nodded.

No wonder Emma had looked so horrified.

It hadn't really been part of the plan, but he hadn't been able to resist seeing if she would recognise him. Just that split second was all it had taken for her to register who she was looking at. And, in an instant, he had gone.

Just like the ghost that he was.

He made his way downstairs, past the faded, framed photographs of Cornish seaside scenes that hung on the wall, and entered the small breakfast area. A young waitress, laying a table, noted his arrival and smiled warmly. He reciprocated.

'Morning, sir,' she said. She sounded Polish, maybe. 'Please, do take a seat. I'll be with you in a minute.'

He nodded and looked around. In the corner an elderly woman was eating alone. Perfect. 'May I join you?' he asked, interrupting her as she buttered some toast.

She looked surprised at first, possibly shocked. There was a free table to her left, where he could have sat in peace.

'I can sit over there,' he said, 'if you'd prefer.'

'Oh, no, no,' she said, her English reserve melting away. 'Please do take a seat. It will be nice to have some company. My husband, he's still in bed asleep, but I've always been an early riser and I couldn't wait for him.' She smiled. 'I was too hungry.'

He slipped into the chair and ordered from the menu.

'Have you been here before?' he asked.

She looked up from her toast. 'Many times. We love Carbis Bay. St Ives is fantastic, but we prefer here – so much quieter, don't you think? – and the beach is amazing. How about you?'

'First time,' he said. 'I'm looking forward to exploring the place.'

'Are you here by yourself?'

'Yes and no. I've got friends staying nearby. But I'm on my own in this place.'

'Well, I've got no doubt you'll have a wonderful time,' she said. 'There's so much to do. Both for the older generation like me and also for you younger folk. And the scenery, well, it's spectacular.'

'I've got my camera,' he said. 'I *love* to take photos.'

'My husband, too,' the woman said. 'He loves his camera. Always snapping away at the sights.'

'I photograph people mostly,' he explained. 'Celebrities. I also collect autographs.' He reached down into the inside pocket of his jacket and pulled out a red notebook. Handing it across the table, he watched as the lady leafed through it.

She seemed impressed. 'You've got . . . a lot of autographs there.' She passed it back to him. 'So, have you and your friends got any plans?'

'Not really. Actually, they don't know I'm here yet.'

She seemed confused. 'Oh, so you're going to surprise them?'

'Yes,' he said. 'It will be a *big* surprise. We haven't seen each other for a long time.'

'Sounds exciting.'

'I hope so.'

They went back to eating. He shovelled in his cooked breakfast. It was tasty and satisfying – just what he needed to set himself up for the day ahead.

When he had finished, he positioned his knife and fork in a cross shape across the empty plate. He thought it was a nice touch, and saw with satisfaction that the woman had noticed.

'You must know this area well,' he said, dabbing the side of his mouth with a napkin.

The lady looked away from his plate. 'Oh, yes, I do.'

'Is there a flower shop nearby?'

'Yes, there is. Bella's Bouquets. Just up on the main road. There's a parade of shops, and it's there. We've used them many times – I like to get flowers for the room. They're very good.'

'Perfect.'

'They're for your friends?'

He nodded. 'It's all part of the surprise.'

'Wonderful!' She smiled. 'I'm sure they'll be thrilled to see you . . .?' She laughed. 'I didn't ask you your name. My name's Ginny.'

'Of course, sorry, I totally forgot. Pleased to meet you, Ginny. My name's Stephen.'

2

Miranda was making breakfast when she heard Edward's raised voice echoing across the house from the study upstairs. She sighed – it wasn't as she'd imagined it would be with Edward, when she had first moved in with him. *Still, for better, for worse,* she thought, drily.

She tried to ignore it, concentrating on preparing the croissants and pains au chocolat. But, after a couple of minutes, she moved out of the kitchen and up the stairs.

By the time she had reached the closed study door, he had quietened down. She knocked. It was the only room in the house, apart from the bathroom, of course, in which she felt such formality was needed. Edward's study was his bolt-hole, and Miranda knew he didn't welcome intrusions, least of all unannounced ones.

'Come in.'

He was sitting at his desk, clutching his mobile phone tightly. Miranda tried a smile, but he didn't return it. She couldn't remember the last time he had been happy. 'Are you okay?'

Edward nodded, although he looked anything but.

She moved towards him and cupped a hand around his shoulder. 'Were you shouting on the phone?'

'A little,' he said, looking down.

'With a client?'

Edward snorted. 'An ex-client.'

'Oh.'

He looked up. '"Oh" indeed.'

'That's the—'

'Third client to leave me in two weeks,' he finished, placing the mobile phone down on the desk. 'That was Clive Monroe. Fifteen years I've been doing his books.'

'I'm so sorry, Edward. What did he say?'

'Oh, same old story – really sorry, but times are hard, gone with an accountancy firm that was offering an introductory deal.'

'Maybe that's the truth.'

Edward shook his head and smiled ruefully. 'People don't want to be associated professionally with someone who has been charged with illegally possessing a gun and inflicting grievous bodily harm.'

'It could be a coincidence.'

He snorted bitterly. 'Miranda, I know you're trying to make me feel better, but it really is so bloody obvious, isn't it?'

She didn't know what to say to that. He was right; it *was* obvious. Since the news had come out that Edward had been charged with shooting Peter Myers during an ill-thought-out attempt to rescue Dan – his appearance in court had been lengthily reported in the papers – he had been fighting a constant battle to hold on to his clients. Many had wobbled and only a few had been convinced to stay – *For now*, thought Miranda grimly – and the danger was clear. His accountancy business relied on his character as much as, if not more than, his accounting skills. What had happened had blown a bullet-shaped hole in how people viewed him.

'I'm worried about you, Edward.'

He stood up impatiently, shrugging off her hold, and paced to the window. 'You should be worried about yourself.'

'What do you mean?'

He turned around. 'You should be worried about how you and the baby are going to survive when I'm either in prison, bankrupt, or both.'

'Edward, don't! It won't come to that.'

'Won't it? I could go to jail for what I did. They nearly charged me with attempted *murder*, for God's sake!'

'But they didn't. They knew there were mitigating circumstances,' Miranda protested. 'The solicitor said so, didn't he? You were under extreme stress. You weren't thinking straight. Anyone can see that it was totally out of character.'

'I *am* guilty, though. I pleaded guilty, stood up there in front of the magistrate and all those other people and admitted it. So I'll be punished by the court, just like I'm being punished by my clients.'

'But the mitigating circumstances – they'll take those into account.'

'Maybe. Or maybe they'll decide to make an example of me.'

'I don't think so.'

'You don't know!' Edward shouted, then checked himself quickly as Miranda shrank back, seeming almost physically wounded by his actions. 'I'm sorry, Miranda, really sorry. I didn't mean to shout, it's just . . .'

'It's just that you're shutting me out, as usual,' Miranda spat, suddenly angry. 'You're trying to deal with this on your own, and cutting me off. You lock yourself away for hours at a time in this room, you don't talk to me about things when you do come out, and the only things I get to know are snippets I overhear from your shouting matches with clients. Well, Edward, I'm sick of it! You might behave as if no one else in the world but you is affected by this situation, but you're *not* on your own.'

'I know, I know,' Edward acknowledged, holding his hands up in conciliation. 'I just . . . I didn't want to worry you, not in your condition.'

Miranda was still fuming. 'I'm pregnant, Edward, not ill. I don't need protecting – even if that were possible, which it isn't. Do you really think you can stop me from worrying, from thinking about what could happen, about what all this might mean for our family?'

'I'm sorry.'

'Do you think I can't see how much this is affecting you? I mean, look at you! I'm sorry to say this, but you look terrible.

You're unshaven half the time, you don't wash. It's clear that something is very wrong.'

Edward closed his eyes and grimaced as if in pain. 'You'd have been much better off not meeting me. You could have met someone your own age, had a family with them and lived a good life.'

Miranda shook her head slowly, disbelievingly. 'You selfish, *selfish* man! Do you know what you're saying? You're saying I'd be better off if this never happened. If *this* never happened.' She gestured at her swollen abdomen.

'I . . . I didn't mean it like that!' Edward backtracked quickly. 'Miranda, I'm sorry.'

But she was past hearing apologies. 'Is this just about the court case, or is it about the baby, too?'

Edward looked shocked. 'I . . . I don't understand.'

'Well, you weren't that overjoyed at the news,' Miranda found herself saying. 'Oh, you said you were happy, but did you look it? I'm not so sure.'

He took a step towards her, arms outstretched. 'Of *course* I'm happy, Miranda. It was a shock at first, yes, but I *am* happy. Once I got used to the idea of being a father again, it felt good.'

Suddenly, Miranda felt the fight leave her as quickly as it had arrived. She shook her head, regretting what she had said, even though she'd meant it. 'Well, Edward,' she said softly, 'you have to show that you're happy, not just say it.'

'I know, I know.' He pulled her towards him and kissed her hair. 'I'm really sorry for everything. I promise I'll try to make things better, for all of us. I truly promise that. Whatever happens, I'll do what it takes.'

She lay on the bed with her eyes closed, still in her pyjamas, thinking about Stuart. She could see his face, hear his voice. How many times had she turned to him for comfort and support? But now he was gone.

What do I have left?

She pulled herself upright and moved over to her dressing table. The jiffy bag was on top, bulging with the volume of material inside.

It had arrived in the post, two days after he had killed himself. She had recognised the handwriting straight away.

And she still couldn't bear to open it. Maybe it was the fear of the unknown, scared of what the package from beyond the grave might contain. *Will there be a suicide note?* She wasn't sure that she wanted to read something like that, even though it might offer an explanation.

She picked up the package. It was a good weight. *A good weight.* She had overheard that comment at Stuart's funeral, muttered by one of the coffin bearers – Alistair, one of Stuart's friends. He hadn't realised that she was standing behind him, and had blushed terribly and apologised.

She thought more about the funeral. All those people offering their condolences, all with the one overriding thought: *It's so sad. I can't believe he's gone.* But those same people, who had been so solemn in the church, had soon recovered their *joie de vivre* at the wake afterwards. She'd watched with growing bitterness as they'd laughed and joked in their small cliques, stuffing themselves with the free food and drink.

Only one person had offered her the support she had needed.

She gazed down again at the package. It was time to open it.

She tore across the top of the seal and shook out the contents of the package onto the surface of the dressing table.

Photographs.

Tears fell as she looked through them. They were from across his life, from young child to recent times.

One image caught her attention.

She lifted it up and gazed at the happy couple.

How did things turn out so badly?

She reached for her mobile phone and dialled the number.

'Hi. It's me . . . Yes, I'm okay, I guess. I was wondering, do you fancy meeting up later? It would be great to see you . . . Fantastic, two o'clock, then. Shall I come over to yours? . . . Great.'

For a few minutes she felt better at the thought of the meet-up, but the injection of positivity was only temporary, and soon she was again wallowing in grief, looking through the photos that Stuart had posted to her.

Why did he send me these?

She pondered that for some time.

And then she spotted what Stuart had done to one of the photographs.

The face of his companion had been scribbled out vigorously using black biro, but she knew who it was. It was then that the realisation hit her. 'Of course.' She walked to the window and looked out across the rooftops. 'I won't let you down, Stuart.'

3

Dan and Emma stayed on the balcony, unspeaking, for a bit longer, enjoying being close to one another. It was so lovely. There hadn't been much physical contact in the past month, and Emma had really missed it. She knew that it wasn't that they didn't want things to happen, but somehow it just didn't seem the right time. She wasn't worried – the lack of sex wasn't surprising, after all they had gone through, and it was early days. Things would get back to how they had been soon, and there was no point rushing things and risking upset.

Emma did wonder whether the holiday away was Dan's attempt to reignite that aspect of their relationship. If it was, she would welcome it.

'How did you sleep?' Dan asked finally. 'You were tossing and turning quite a bit at one point.'

Emma raised her head from his chest. 'Is that what woke you up?'

'No. I'd been awake for a while already. I was thinking about something.'

She waited for him to elaborate, but he didn't. 'Want to share?'

Dan hesitated for a second or two. 'I was thinking about Peter Myers.'

She sat up in surprise. 'Really? What about him?'

Another hesitation. 'I was wondering how he is – what he's doing.'

His admission came as a shock. They'd hardly spoken the man's name since being reunited. 'You're *concerned* about him?'

'Maybe,' Dan replied. 'I don't know. I know what he did was terrible, but at the heart of it, he's a victim, too.'

'Because of what happened to Stephen?'

Dan nodded, taking a sip of coffee. 'Who knows how you'd react if you found out that your son or daughter had been murdered? Maybe you'd want to take revenge, too. Maybe the anger would twist your morals, lead you to doing something you wouldn't normally contemplate.'

'I can see that,' she replied, a little doubtfully.

'I know it sounds crazy, empathising with him, but I can see how he might have got to where he is now.' Dan shrugged.

'I don't think it sounds crazy.'

'He'll go to prison for many years.'

Peter Myers had been charged with a raft of offences, including kidnapping and grievous bodily harm. He'd pleaded guilty to all charges and had been remanded in custody, pending sentencing. There was little doubt that he would spend a long time behind bars for what he'd done; the sentence would have been longer if Richard hadn't survived the series of blows to his head that had left him fighting for his life. But he had come out of his coma, thankfully, without any long-term damage, and was now up in Edinburgh, staying with friends, continuing his recovery and recuperation.

'You do think Peter Myers deserves to be punished though, don't you?' Emma said.

'Oh, yes, of course I do. He deserves to go to jail for what he did – there's no doubt about that. It's just that, well . . . it's complicated.'

Emma breathed an inward sigh of relief. Although she could certainly see where Dan was coming from, it was still uncomfortable hearing him say supportive things about Peter Myers. It reminded her of that so-called Stockholm syndrome, where captives began to empathise with, and even support, their captors.

'Anyway, you didn't answer my original question,' Dan added. 'About how you slept. I'm worried about you, too, you know.'

'I had another nightmare,' Emma revealed.

Dan looked concerned. 'About Stephen Myers?'

Emma nodded. 'It was the same dream, the wedding.'

'I'm sorry,' Dan said.

'Why are you apologising? It's not your fault.'

'Maybe it is.'

'What do you mean?'

'Well, it was my idea to postpone the wedding. Maybe that's why you keep dreaming about it.'

'It was for the best,' Emma replied. 'We agreed.'

Three days after Dan was freed from Peter Myers' lair, they had been at home watching television when Emma had broached the subject of when they should get married. Dan's thought that it would be best to wait had taken her by surprise.

They had missed the original date, of course, but Emma had expected that they would marry as soon as practicably possible. She had been prepared to strip back the wedding to the bare bones to get it sorted more quickly, and had told him so. But he had said he didn't want to rush it, and that if they did, she might regret it later.

'I know, but I wonder whether I pushed you into it,' Dan said. 'Maybe we should have just gone ahead and got married as soon as we could.'

Emma shook her head. 'No. It was the right thing to do. Yes, of course I want to be married to you, right now. That's how it was supposed to be. But you were right. It would have been no good to get married when there are still all these things going on – Richard is still recuperating, Dad is worried sick about the court case, and the rest of us . . . you, me, Will and Lizzy – we're all still coming to terms with what happened. That's not a good time to get married, is it?'

'No, it isn't,' Dan agreed.

Emma was particularly concerned about her father. He'd been charged with illegal possession of a firearm and grievous bodily harm with intent, following his shooting of Peter Myers in his attempt to rescue Dan. The authorities had considered charging him with attempted murder, because of the use of the gun, but had decided on the lesser charge. *Thank God he only wounded him.* But Edward had, nevertheless, responded very badly to the charges.

Dan continued. 'But I *am* worried about you, Em. These dreams about Stephen Myers, I don't like them at all. It's like he's back, stalking you.'

'He's dead,' Emma stated. 'It's my imagination, that's all.'

'Like yesterday at the motorway services in Exeter?'

Emma nodded, reluctantly. En route to Cornwall, they had stopped at the Moto Motorway Services in Exeter, just off the M5, to buy some lunch and stretch their legs. The mild, sunny October weather, with temperatures into the early seventies predicted for the week ahead, had no doubt attracted many more people to journey down. The car park had been filled with all manner of vehicles loaded with surfboards, walking gear and camping equipment.

It was as she had exited the toilets that Emma had seen the man. He was standing with his back to her, on the other side of the atrium, near the slot machines. And then he had turned one hundred and eighty degrees, and had appeared to look straight at her.

She had caught her breath at the sight of his face.

It was Stephen Myers.

Except it wasn't. Because Stephen Myers was dead.

Instinctively she had looked away, unable to face that ghoul from the past. When she had turned back, he had gone.

'It did shake me up,' Emma said now.

Of course, she knew that it had just been her mind playing tricks on her. The person had looked like Stephen Myers, or how she remembered him. But it felt as if, for that moment, he had been there, living and breathing.

Not dead, but *alive.*

'I can imagine,' Dan replied. 'I'm glad you told me about it.' He looked at her. 'You need to feel that you can tell me anything that's happening, as that's how we're going to get through this.'

Emma nodded, slowly. In fact, she *had* considered not telling him, but Dan had spotted straight away that something was wrong. And he was right. Because it hadn't been the first time she'd thought she'd seen Stephen Myers. A week earlier, while out shopping with Lizzy on Oxford Street, a man had brushed past her in John Lewis. She'd caught only the briefest of glimpses of his face but, as at the services, her initial reaction had been that it was him. Even though it couldn't have been.

She exhaled. 'I'm starting to think I'm going mad.'

'It's just a natural reaction to an amazingly stressful situation,' Dan said. 'You're not crazy.'

'Hopefully not. I think it's just all been getting too much. That's why this holiday was such a great idea – it gives us a chance to really get away from everything and clear our heads.'

'Definitely,' Dan agreed. 'Maybe we shouldn't talk about any of this while we're here. Just pretend that it never happened, and enjoy the next few days.'

Emma smiled. 'As man and wife?'

He grinned. 'Why not? Mr and Mrs Carlton, on their honeymoon.'

'Sounds like a fantastic idea.'

'That's because it is,' Dan said, smiling.

'So, what's the plan for today, Mr Carlton?'

'Well, Mrs Carlton, shall we go over there?' he said, pointing towards St Ives. It was still bathed in sunshine. 'The weather's perfect. And I've heard there are some seriously good places to eat, drink and shop.'

'Sounds great,' Emma said, planting a kiss on his cheek.

Dan sat back in his chair and finished his coffee, which by now was cold. Emma had gone to shower, and he'd promised to prepare breakfast. But he felt paralysed, unable to banish the worries from his mind. Looking out over the sparkling seascape, he searched for some release.

He should tell her.

He *wanted* to tell her.

To admit to her what he feared the most.

4

Before leaving her flat, Lizzy gazed in the mirror for the last time, running a hand through her strawberry-blonde hair. She looked tired. The past few weeks had been difficult, trying to get over her nightmare-like experience while also continuing her lead role in the sixties musical, *Like We Did Last Summer*. They had given her a couple of weeks off, and offered her more, but she'd insisted on returning: it wouldn't do her any good to have too much time to think about events; it was much better to carry on as normal. Plus, it wasn't good to relinquish a role in a successful production – the musical, set in the swinging sixties, had been playing to packed houses since opening. So, two weeks ago, she had returned to the lead role.

It had felt good, but it was exhausting – it didn't help that she wasn't sleeping well. Usually she could fall asleep anywhere – on top of a pinhead, her mother had once said – but it hadn't been like that recently. Many times she'd woken in a panic, thinking that she was still in Peter Myers' house, blindfolded and tied to a chair. She'd taken up the police victim support officer's offer of counselling, and that was helping, but she knew it would take time, even for someone as strong as she was. It was the same for all of them – they were all going through the same thing, in one way or another.

But there was one thing in particular that gnawed at her – what Peter Myers had told her during the first few hours of her imprisonment.

It was something she'd never tell anyone, perhaps not even admit to herself.

★　　★　　★

Lizzy exited the flat and paced towards the bus stop. It was a beautiful, sunny autumn day and she wished she'd remembered her sunglasses. Only moments after she had arrived at the stop, her bus drew up at it, and she sent up a quick, silent prayer of thanks to the travel gods as she stepped on.

The West End-bound bus was crowded, but there was a free seat towards the back. A man who had also been waiting at the stop – he'd arrived just after she had – sat down next to her. He was in his middle to late thirties, with a receding hairline.

'Nice day,' he said.

'Yes,' Lizzy replied, glancing up from her stage notes and groaning inwardly. Normally ready to talk to strangers, today she felt unsociable. Apart from anything else, she really needed the time on the bus to revise her lines. She'd been quite forgetful since returning to the stage. Only little things – a line that came out slightly wrong, or a hesitation at who was supposed to be speaking next – but she was a perfectionist, and it wasn't acceptable, not on the London stage. And although her fellow cast members had been too polite to mention the slip-ups, the director certainly hadn't. He'd been supportive, acknowledging that it was understandable given what she'd been through but, at the same time, he had made it clear that he expected her to address the issue pretty quickly, or stand aside.

She could understand that.

'It's Lizzy, isn't it?' the man said.

Lizzy stiffened. 'How do you—?'

'It's okay,' he interrupted. 'Don't be alarmed. I know it looks weird, but I only want a quick chat. I thought the bus ride would be the perfect opportunity.'

Now Lizzy was angry. She recognised the voice. 'It's *you*, isn't it?'

'Yes,' he said, proffering a hand. 'Adrian Spencer, *Daily Post*.'

Lizzy wanted to push past him and sit somewhere else. For the past three weeks, this guy had been calling her, asking for an interview. He was writing a feature article about the events surrounding Dan's kidnap. Lizzy, like Emma and the others, had refused his increasingly persistent advances. 'You've got some nerve.'

He shrugged. 'You have to, in my job.'

'Well, it's not a job I'd want to do, harassing people who have been through terrible events and who are just trying to get on with their lives.'

'Steady on,' he said. 'Harassment is a bit strong.'

'You think so? Well, where I come from, what you've been doing – calling me, Emma, Will, Dan, Richard, Edward numerous times, not taking no for an answer, and now pestering me on my way to work – is definitely harassment. And if you don't stop it, I *will* call the police, you understand?'

'Okay, okay.' The reporter shrugged and attempted an appeasing smile. 'I appreciate that you could see it in that way, but I just want to get the story straight. I'll be writing the article whether I speak to you or not, so surely it's better for you to get your side of the story? You wouldn't want to be misrepresented, would you?'

Lizzy bristled. 'Don't threaten me.'

He laughed that off. 'Now, come on, I'm not threatening anyone. It's just a fact. My editor wants to run this story, the readers want to read about it, so it's going to happen. How it happens is up to you, in many ways.'

'Okay,' Lizzy said. 'I'll give you a quote.'

'Great, let me just get my recorder.' He delved into his pocket and brought out a digital recording device, pressing the record button as he held it between them. 'Feel free to go ahead.'

'Get lost!'

Adrian Spencer's face creased and he lowered the device. 'I can see that now isn't a good time.'

'Let me get this straight,' Lizzy said. 'It will *never* be a good time. You won't get anything from me.'

'Not even for a fee?'

Lizzy laughed. 'You must be desperate, if you're starting to offer money. The answer's no, not for any amount. You understand?'

'I still don't see why you're so hostile about this.'

She shook her head. This man just didn't get it. 'Because, as I've explained to you several times over the phone, what happened to us isn't entertainment. We're all still coming to terms with what happened, it's extremely difficult and stressful, and we don't want our lives served up in your crappy newspaper just to satisfy people's curiosity.'

A couple of the passengers had pricked up their ears, chancing a glance as Lizzy's tone sharpened. She ignored their looks.

Adrian smirked. 'Can I quote you on that?'

'Screw you. Now, please move.' The bus was still some way from her stop, but she decided it was time to leave. She would gladly walk the extra minutes to get away from this creep.

He stood up to let her pass, but as she disembarked he followed her off the bus at the corner of Shaftsbury Avenue.

'Leave me alone,' she shouted, as the bus pulled away. 'Don't you understand English?'

'Sure, I'll leave you alone,' he said. 'But there's one last thing before I go.'

'I don't want to hear it.' Lizzy started walking away.

'I think you do,' he shouted after her. 'I know your secret. I know all about what Peter Myers told you.'

Lizzy stopped and turned round.

Edward waited in his car in the suburban London road, his eyes trained on the house opposite. Clive Monroe's silver-grey Volvo was in the drive, so he had to be at home – Clive didn't walk anywhere. He glanced at himself in the rear-view mirror. Miranda was right – he looked terrible. *Am I doing the right thing?* He had left Miranda at home, making an excuse about needing to meet a different client – a client who hadn't just dumped him.

Taking a steadying breath, he got out, locked the vehicle, crossed the street and rapped on the door.

Clive, in a too-small green golf shirt that clung to his belly, looked shocked and then defensive as he opened the door. 'Edward. Why have you—?'

'I wanted to discuss things face to face.'

Clive shook his head, looking towards his feet and revealing his expanding bald spot. 'I'm really sorry, Edward, but I explained everything on the phone. I've made my decision.'

'I hoped I might be able to change your mind.'

Clive looked pained. 'As I said, times are hard. The kitchen appliance business isn't what it used to be. I've cut costs across the company, and this is just another decision I've had to take.'

'Fifteen years, Clive. It's been *fifteen* years.'

'I know, I know, but—'

'My charges are very reasonable. Switching to someone new for an introductory offer can't have saved you much. A few hundred pounds, maybe?'

Clive's face gave him the answer.

'Is it worth it?' Edward pressed. 'I mean, I know your business inside out. How much money have I saved you over the years, because I understand what you do? More than a few hundred pounds, that's for certain.'

Clive was clearly embarrassed – he could hardly look Edward in the face – but he wasn't budging. 'I'm sorry, Edward.' He went to close the door.

'Clive! Whatever this company has quoted you, I'll match it.'

'Sorry.'

Edward placed his foot in the doorway. 'I'll undercut it by ten per cent. Can't say fairer than that. And I'll honour that price for the next three years.'

'Please, Edward, it's not just about—' Clive Monroe stopped himself.

Edward shook his head. 'The money. It's not just about the money. That's what you were going to say, wasn't it?'

Clive opened the door a little wider. 'I didn't want to have to have this conversation.'

'You don't want me to do your books because of what's happening with the court case,' Edward stated flatly.

Clive nodded.

Edward ran a hand across his face. 'Hell, Clive, thanks for the support.'

Clive looked up and down the street, as if he was checking to see if any neighbours might overhear. 'It's not like that. I *do* support you, Edward. Christ, if I'd been in your position, then I might have done the same thing. You did well not to blow that guy's head off, after what he put your daughter through.'

Edward held out his hands. 'So why dump me?'

'Because I think you need some time out, to focus on getting through this.'

Edward scoffed. 'You're doing this for *my* benefit? That's a really poor excuse, Clive.'

Clive shrugged. 'All I can say is sorry.'

Edward stared at him. 'Do you realise what will happen if all my clients do what you're doing? I'll have nothing left – absolutely *nothing*!'

Clive raised his chin. 'You're a fantastic accountant, Edward. But you're not in the right place at the moment. I mean, look at what you're doing right now – door-stepping me, refusing to take no for an answer, raising your voice. You're not yourself.'

'I'm not raising my voice!' Edward checked himself, and suddenly the fight went out of him. 'Just forget it.' He sighed. 'Goodbye, Clive.'

He trudged back to the car and sat hugging the steering wheel. His reputation and business were in freefall.

Edward opened his wallet and pulled out the contact card the man had given him.

I promise I'll try to make things better, for all of us.

He stared at the telephone number.

I truly promise that. Whatever happens, I'll do what it takes.

He keyed in the number. On the second ring he cut the call. His chest was tightening. Reaching into the glovebox, he grabbed his angina spray and inhaled. Almost immediately he felt better, but he still felt short of breath. It was nerves. Taking some time to steady himself, he breathed deeply as he gazed out of the window at the cars passing by.

Was this a terrible mistake?

His thoughts turned to Miranda and the baby, and the devastating impact that the current crisis could have on all their lives.

Gathering his resolve, he keyed in the number again. This time he waited for the pick-up. 'Hello. It's Edward Holden. I'm ready to talk.'

5

Will Holden sat down on the park bench, stretched out his legs and looked up at the clear, blue sky. Overhead, a plane trailed across, en route to Heathrow. He brought his vision back down to earth, scanning Regent's Park. It was still early morning, just past ten, but already the autumn sun and mild temperatures had begun to bring out the weekend crowds. There were the usual joggers, a mixture of ages and sizes, pounding the grass and paths, plugged into their music players, lost in their own world; there were the dog walkers – a heavily built, skin-headed man strode past with an equally muscly bull mastiff; there were the families, children playing with balls or engaged in chase with their siblings; and there were the lovers, hand in hand, out for a morning stroll.

Will smiled. Things felt good. Just a few weeks ago – in this very same park – it had been so different. The sense of doom had been suffocating as he had wondered whether Dan was still alive, and whether everything that was happening was because of him, because of what he had done.

And it had been.

Or at least what he had been party to. Yes, it was Stuart Harris who had killed Stephen Myers – Will had learnt only later that he had planted a knife in his side and watched him bleed to death – but it was Will who had helped him to dispose of the body, after Stuart had told him a different story and reminded him that they were soon to be in-laws. Will had driven across the country with the stiffening corpse wrapped in sheets in the back of his car. He, along with Stuart, had parked by the deserted canal side and dropped Stephen Myers into the water.

He hadn't been forced to do it. Stuart had begged him to help, yes, but there had been a choice. He could have called the police there and then, rather than embroiling himself in all the horror. And then, with the deed done, it was he who had kept quiet about what had happened, telling only his father, who had sworn him to secrecy. Will still regretted keeping the secret for so long.

It had been such a relief to tell Emma and the others the truth.

They had persuaded him not to tell the police. They had been clear – admitting his crime to the authorities wouldn't achieve anything, apart from punishing him even more than he had already punished himself.

In the aftermath of Dan's rescue, he had considered what to do. And he had decided that they were right. The burden of hiding the secret had been lifted – for the first time in years, he felt free of its crushing weight.

He had been given another chance.

Suddenly he saw Amy, walking across the grass, her arms swinging lightly at her sides as she approached. She was wearing tracksuit bottoms and a T-shirt. She looked beautiful, with her blonde hair tied back into a ponytail and her lightly freckled face catching the light.

'Hi,' she said, smiling. 'You're early.'

'So are you.' Will smiled back, standing to greet her. She offered him her cheek and he kissed it lightly.

They had met two and a half weeks ago at a bar in town. Amy had sparked up conversation while waiting to get served and, for the next two hours, they'd talked non-stop about all manner of things – their backgrounds, likes and dislikes, hopes for the future. She was a sports teacher at an inner-city comprehensive school, and obviously loved her job. Will had never met anyone so instantly attractive – looks as well as personality-wise – so he'd been amazed when she had suggested meeting up the next day for a coffee.

Just over a fortnight and numerous dates later, things couldn't have been going any better.

'Are you ready, then,' she said, 'to face your fears?'

Will nodded.

At their first meeting he had revealed his fear of spiders, and how it was the main barrier to him visiting his old school friend, Ed, who had emigrated to Australia three years ago. Ed and his wife, Yvonne, had invited him there numerous times, but the thought of visiting a country where spiders came as big as your fist was just too much.

For as long as he could remember, he'd hated spiders. It probably had something to do with the film *Arachnophobia*, which he had watched at a friend's house when he was only ten years old. The movie, about a town plagued by arachnids, had lingered in his memory.

On their third date – a moonlit walk by the Thames – Amy had suggested a radical treatment for his fear: holding a tarantula as part of a phobia treatment session at London Zoo. She knew a friend who had done it, and it had worked really well.

After first dismissing the idea due to sheer horror, Will had come around. At the heart of it, he wanted to impress Amy, who was obviously much more adventurous than he – she had been trekking in Nepal, explored South America on a gap year by herself, regularly parachute jumped – Will was afraid of heights – and had competed in several triathlons, to name just some of her exploits. Compared to all of that, holding a spider in a controlled environment seemed straightforward.

Except that it wasn't, of course.

Now, they walked hand in hand across the grass towards the entrance to London Zoo. Suddenly, Will wanted to back out. And his face must have shown it.

'Are you sure you're okay?' Amy said, as they reached the gates. 'You look, well, terrible.'

'I'm fine,' he lied. 'Just a bit nervous.'

Amy smiled warmly. 'It's okay, you know – you don't have to do this. Don't feel forced into it. We could try again another time.'

Will braced himself. He had to do this now, or it would never happen. There would never be a better chance. 'No, I'm doing it.'

They paid at the desk and entered the zoo. It was another ten minutes until their slot for the up-close and personal session with the spider, so they spent the time wandering around, Amy trying to take Will's mind off the impending encounter. They spent time watching the penguins, where Amy revealed that she intended to visit Antarctica – she had already done some investigating of possible options. Her distraction technique worked and by the time they headed off to the building, Will felt better. A little bit.

Ten minutes later and Will was standing, Amy by his side, with the biggest spider he had ever seen being lowered gently onto the palm of his hand.

The keeper stood back as he brought his hand away from the tarantula.

'Are you okay, Will?'

Will nodded, not daring to breathe in case it startled the spider into scurrying up his arm, or jumping towards his face. Suddenly his arms didn't seem long enough. But a few small breaths and he suddenly realised he *was* okay, watching the creature with its hairy black legs as it moved slowly over his palm.

'Its legs tickle,' he said finally, managing to get some words out.

The man nodded. 'He's a friendly chap, Horace. Likes giving massages to make people feel comfortable.'

The spider paused, as if wondering what to do. Will looked across at Amy, who smiled.

'There's no doubt,' the man said, 'that lots of people are afraid of spiders. My wife nearly split up with me when she realised what I did for a living – she was scared stiff that one might stow away in my bag and appear in front of her. But now she's fine with them, and most people are, if you can break down the instinctive barrier that's there.'

Will focused on the spider again. Holding it was a lot better than he'd expected, although obviously he was still nervous. 'Do a lot of people do this kind of thing?'

'A lot. Since we started doing these sessions a few years ago, the number of people enrolling has grown every year.'

'Does anyone ever freak out, when you first bring out the spider?'

'Some do,' the keeper acknowledged. 'One man, a banker from the City, came in here last week, all bravado, until he saw Horace. He couldn't leave the building quickly enough. But mostly people warm to them, once they realise that there's really nothing to be scared of. After all, even the bigger spiders are much smaller than we are.'

Will felt a sense of achievement – he could have been one of those people who had lost it, turned on his heel and run. But he hadn't. He'd faced his fears, kept his cool and come through. It felt good, really good.

'Had enough?' the man asked. 'Or would you like to meet Horace's friend? He's a little bit bigger than this guy, and faster.'

Will looked over at Amy again, then back at the man. 'Why not?'

6

He left the flower shop feeling very satisfied, and sauntered back down the hill with the camera around his neck, towards the gated seaside holiday apartments where Emma and Dan were staying. *This is all going to plan so far.* As he got closer, he checked himself, slowing his pace and scanning the streets carefully as he went. He didn't want to run into them yet. The big reveal shouldn't come too soon.

He reached the complex, and paused at the iron security gate. Looking through into the car park, he could see their car. That didn't mean they were in, though. He crossed over the street and glanced up quickly towards the apartment on the end, overlooking the road – having scouted it out the previous evening, he knew it was theirs. They weren't on the balcony, but there was a light on. Then he saw someone moving inside.

It was her. He turned quickly, for fear of being spotted, and headed further down the hill.

And then he saw his first target.

She was perfect. Around the right kind of age – mid to late twenties. Pretty. A jogger, too. A blonde though, instead of a brunette, although he suspected that the tied-back hair was bottle-blonde rather than natural. She came out of a side road just down from Emma's apartment complex, wearing a black tracksuit with gold trim and clutching a sports-style water bottle in her hand. He didn't think that she'd seen him as she ran off left, down towards the coast. She certainly hadn't given him a second look.

He fired off a couple of shots with his camera and admired his handiwork. And then he started to half jog and half walk after her, leaving enough of a gap so as not to arouse suspicion. He knew the railway station was at the bottom of the hill, so anyone seeing him would probably assume he was running for a train. He picked up the pace slightly, as she was now some distance away – he thought he knew where she was going, but he couldn't be sure, and didn't want to lose contact.

Losing the first one would be disappointing.

'So, how does it feel?' Amy said, taking a sip from her coffee, sitting across from Will in the zoo's restaurant. 'Conquering your fears like that?'

'It feels brilliant,' Will replied. 'Absolutely brilliant.' He still couldn't quite believe that he had done it. Before today, he wouldn't have dared pick up anything larger than a money spider but there he had been, cradling a tarantula. And to think that that morning he had been so close to calling Amy and making an excuse – thank goodness his desire to impress had won out over his fears. Now he felt empowered, and it was all thanks to the beautiful girl sitting opposite him.

Amy smiled. 'But how did you feel when you first saw the spider?'

'Scared, really scared.'

'And when the guy lowered it onto your hand?'

Will shuddered. It would take time before he was fully comfortable with doing something like that. 'Terrified.'

Amy nodded. 'That's how I felt.'

Will was taken aback. 'What? I didn't know you were scared of spiders.'

'I don't mean then. I mean every time I've done something challenging. The first parachute jump, I was scared witless. Those first few days in South America, when I realised I really was out there on my own, just me and my rucksack, were dreadful. On the second day I nearly booked a flight straight back home.'

'I didn't realise. I thought . . .'

41

'That I was fearless?' Amy grinned. 'Far from it. I forced myself to do all those things. To me, it's not a challenge if you're not frightened, even just a little bit.' She popped a spoonful of froth from her cappuccino into her mouth. 'Life is filled with things to be afraid of so, as far as I can see it, you've got a choice – either you run away from them, or you face them down. And, from my experience, it's a lot more fun facing them head-on.'

'You're amazing,' Will found himself saying out loud. He blushed.

'Thanks,' she said, seemingly not embarrassed at all by his statement. 'I think you're pretty amazing too, Will Holden.'

'No one's ever called me pretty amazing before,' Will joked, glad to be able to defuse his discomfort with humour. A contented silence fell, and he thought about something as he stirred his drink.

'Amy, why are you here, with me?'

'Pardon?' she said, confused. 'I don't understand.'

'Why are you here, with me?' he repeated. 'Why aren't you with someone else?'

She seemed to realise what he meant. 'Because I want to be with you,' she said, simply.

Will didn't look satisfied.

'Isn't that enough?' she said. 'I mean, I could ask the same of you – why are you with me this sunny Saturday morning? Why aren't *you* with someone else?'

Will nodded. 'Fair point.' He looked at her. 'It's just that, well, I don't want to embarrass you, but, you know, you're so . . . beautiful. And you're great company. I'm surprised you weren't already with someone else.'

Amy hadn't spoken about her previous relationships, and Will hadn't probed until now. But he had wondered.

Amy's forehead creased for a microsecond, and Will regretted bringing up the subject and risking this lovely day. 'I'm sorry, I'm being nosy. It's none of my business.'

'No, it's okay,' she said.

Is she tearing up?

She recovered quickly. 'I've had relationships, yes. But that's all in the past.' She sipped again at her coffee.

There were a few painful seconds of silence this time. Will decided to change topic. 'So, you said about explaining what's next.'

'Oh, yes,' she said, perking up. 'We can't be late for our flight.'

'Flight?'

She reached down into her bag and pulled out a white envelope, which she placed on the table. 'Will Holden, are you ready to face your next fear?'

It sounded like he was taking part in a game show. Will fought his instinctive reaction, which was to ask questions to find out more about it all. He trusted Amy, and would go along with whatever she had planned. 'Yes.'

'Excellent,' she said, 'otherwise the tickets would have been wasted.'

'Please don't say it's a parachute jump.'

She raised an eyebrow. 'And what would you say if I said it was?'

Will felt sick at the thought. 'Well, I guess I've already said yes.'

'Damn.' She thumped the table playfully. 'I should have aimed higher.'

Will's forehead creased in confusion.

'Open the envelope,' she said. 'It's not a parachute jump – that will have to wait. But full marks for being up for it.'

Will slid his fingers under the seal of the envelope. Inside were two tickets for the London Eye.

He had mentioned his fear of heights during their first discussion at the bar where they'd met, and had actually referenced London's big wheel as one of the things he didn't feel able to do. Eighteen months before, Emma, Dan and Lizzy had gone on it, and he'd watched from below, feeling left out, thoroughly miserable and full of self-loathing for his inadequacies. And when they had disembarked, enthusing about the amazing sight from the top, he'd felt so jealous. So although it wasn't a parachute jump, it was another leap for him.

He looked up at Amy, whose blue eyes were sparkling at him. 'I'll do it.'

He had been right about her destination: the beach. He watched from a wall that ran along the edge of the sand as she jogged along the otherwise deserted shoreline. For the next ten minutes he fired off dozens and dozens of shots as she began doing shuttle-runs up and down the sand.

He admired the covert images that he had captured. That was the thrill. The voyeurism of it all. This girl, whoever she was, didn't know that a little part of her had been taken.

She stopped her runs and, hands on hips, looked out to sea. He did likewise, noticing for the first time the sound of the waves crashing, the mild coastal breeze and the beauty of the water as it sparkled in the sunlight. Bringing the camera back up to his eye, he took three more snaps. The last one was the best – the girl, with golden sand in the foreground, framed in the background by the sparkling water. It was quite stunning. Suddenly, he longed to speak to the girl, find out what she was like, *who* she was. He had the images, but not the person.

Maybe he should approach her ...

'Oi, mate!'

He spun round, nearly dropping the camera in his shock. His questioner was a lifeguard, an athletically built guy in his early twenties with shaggy, surfer-dude hair, pushing six foot three, maybe four.

'What are you doing?' he asked in a broad Cornish accent, nodding towards the camera.

'Er, taking photos,' he replied.

'Of what?' His tone wasn't at all friendly.

Has he been watching?

'The beach, and the sea.'

'Really?'

'Yes, I photograph landscapes,' he said, recovering his composure. 'That's why I come down here, because the scenery is just so beautiful.'

'Mind if I take a look?'

He thought quickly. To refuse would look too suspicious. He swallowed his concerns. 'Of course.'

He clicked back to the final image, hoping that it would suffice.

'Sure is beautiful,' the guy said. 'Mind if I take a look at some more?'

Feeling there was no other option, he passed across the camera, which still hung from his neck, and watched as the guy clicked through image after image – they were all of the girl, who was still standing at the water's edge.

The guy passed the camera back. 'Do you know her?'

'I'm sorry?'

'Do you know her? The girl you've been photographing?'

'I . . .'

'I've been watching you for the past ten minutes,' the lifeguard continued. 'You don't know her, do you?'

He looked down. 'No.'

'Then I think you need to delete those photos, don't you?'

'I didn't mean any harm.'

'Just delete them, mate.'

He did as requested. By now, the girl was coming back across the sand.

'I really should tell Kirsty about this,' the guy said. 'She's a friend of mine.'

He watched her coming closer and felt panic. 'Please, don't. Please, I'm really sorry.'

She was now within shouting distance.

'Hey, Kirsty!' the guy shouted. 'Can you come over here for a second? I just want to introduce you to someone.'

But he didn't wait to hear her response. He turned and fled back up the hill without looking back.

He sprinted around the corner and came to an exhausted stop next to a phone box. Bent over at the waist, he slowed his breathing and thought about what had just happened. It had been embarrassing, not to mention foolish – what if that guy had insisted on calling the police? It would have made things extremely complicated. *How would I have explained my actions?* He looked up suddenly. *Maybe he has called them.* He took a step round the back of the phone box, so that he was hidden from the main road.

'That was really *stupid*,' he said out loud, looking skyward. 'So stupid. Something that . . .' *But of course!* He smiled to himself at a sudden realisation. 'It was okay.'

The whole scenario, it had been *perfect*. He couldn't have planned it any better.

Dwelling on his good fortune, he forgot about the possibility the police might come looking for the strange man who had been stalking women on the beach. He looked at his watch, smiled again and then headed back up towards the holiday apartments. He was almost ready.

7

'This is amazing,' Emma said, as she walked hand in hand with Dan down towards the seafront. The five-minute train ride from their base to the main resort of St Ives had been breathtaking. The line arced around the golden coast, hugging the cliffs and offering a spectacular view across the bay and out to sea.

'Yes, amazing.' Dan was watching a flock of seagulls that was circling overhead before allowing the wind to carry them away into the far distance. The sun was still shining in a clear blue sky, and it felt as if he and Emma had stepped into a vivid oil painting.

They strolled through a quaint alleyway of micro-galleries, restaurants and boutique shops. Dan held up the town-centre map that they'd picked up from their apartment. 'The main beach is the next right.'

'Wouldn't it be amazing,' Emma said, as she peered into the window of a shop that sold beautiful knitwear, 'to own a shop like this? Just move out of London, come down here and live the quiet life. Early morning seafront walks, fresh air, no stress.'

Dan moved up to her shoulder. 'Is that what you'd really like to do?'

She shrugged. 'Sure, why not?'

'Sounds idyllic, but I thought London was the place to be for those in the' – he put on a mock posh accent, as opposed to his usual South Yorkshire twang – '*acting* profession.'

Emma elbowed him playfully in the ribs. 'Plenty of actors live in the countryside, you know. I've heard Gloucestershire, the Cotswolds, is full of them – Kate Winslet, for example.'

'Ah, but Gloucestershire is about an hour and a half's train ride from London, or a short drive in a fast car, while St Ives, Cornwall – well, it's a lot further away.'

'True,' Emma acknowledged. 'But if I wasn't acting, it wouldn't matter.'

'Really?' Dan said. 'You're not thinking of walking away from it all, are you?'

'Maybe.'

'Because of what happened?'

'Partly, yes.' Emma was still wounded by the way the casting director Guy Roberts had behaved. He had offered her an audition for a film without telling her that he had done it as a favour for her ex-fiancé, Stuart Harris. Although Guy claimed that his subsequent decision to then cast her in the film had been made purely on the grounds that she was right for the part, the deception still grated. Once again, Emma felt the rightness of her decision to reject his offer of the lead female role – when she had learnt that Guy had used Dan's kidnapping as a means of generating publicity for the film, she had wanted nothing to do with it, and still didn't: she still couldn't get over the fact that he had paid a freelance photographer to follow her and take photographs, which were then placed in the tabloid press. The whole incident had made the nightmare of Dan's disappearance even more unbearable. And Guy had seemed completely unrepentant. 'I'm just not sure if I want to be part of all that any more.'

Emma expected Dan to come back with a reason why she shouldn't even contemplate the thought of giving up her acting career, but he didn't. 'Are you going to say anything to Diana about how you're feeling?'

'No,' Emma replied. 'I'm just going to listen to what she has to say.'

She was meeting Diana Saunders, a prospective new agent on Wednesday, the day after they were due to return from holiday. Diana had contacted her out of the blue a week before, wanting to discuss taking her on as a client as part of a potential 'amazing opportunity', as she had put it. She had refused to elaborate, quoting a confidentiality clause that restricted her saying too much over the telephone. Emma had strongly suspected that was a lie but, still, the hook had worked and she had agreed to a meeting despite her reservations.

'You're still not convinced that she's right for you?' Dan asked.

Emma turned back to looking in the shop window. 'I guess I can't make that judgement until I've met her. But it's just that with her reputation – fearsome and ruthless – well, she doesn't sound like the sort of person I'd normally get along with.'

Dan moved across and leant on the window ledge. His attention was caught by two youngsters zipping past on scooters. 'Not as a friend, definitely. But as an *agent*, maybe. I mean, she might be just the sort of person you need batting for you, to protect you from people like Guy Roberts.'

'True.' Diana had been charming on the phone, and extremely persuasive – which surely had to be an agent's most important trait. She could be just the person Emma needed.

And what harm can one meeting do, even if it doesn't work out?

'I mean, there are nasty people in every walk of life, in every profession.' Dan reached over to gently pull Emma down to sit beside him. 'Sometimes we deal with clients who are awful, and you're just glad that you don't work for them all the time. Remember that guy who I went over to see at his offices, and he was just so mean to his female assistant? I couldn't believe it.'

It was true. Dan, working as a web designer in a small but highly successful company in the capital, had told Emma about many horrible clients in the past.

'I know. I shouldn't forget that nastiness isn't confined to the entertainment industry. And Diana contacting me, it couldn't be better timing.' Emma's long-standing agent had just announced her retirement.

'Do you think she knows? That you're without an agent?'

Emma hadn't thought of that possibility before now. 'Maybe. I guess she must have a lot of contacts.'

They stood up and carried on walking, hand in hand. 'You know, Em, I'll support you in whatever you decide to do, but just make sure you do it for the right reasons. If you really want to move down here and live the rural seaside life, I'll be with you all the way. I mean, I could go freelance. With web design, it doesn't matter where you live if you're freelance – it's just about building up a reputation, and you can work with people anywhere in the world. But don't let what happened scare you into giving up your dreams.'

Emma stopped and hugged him. 'Thanks. I won't.'

Then, while still in the embrace, over Dan's shoulder, she saw something down the road.

Some*one*.

She froze in Dan's arms.

It can't be? Can it?

Dan sensed her stiffen and he pulled back. 'What's the matter?'

Emma peered up towards the top of the street again. A man was standing up near the crossroads, looking her way. She couldn't see his face properly – it was just too far away. But there was something about him – his outline maybe, the way he stood . . . and then she saw him lift something towards his face, again in her direction.

A camera!

'It's him,' she breathed.

'Who?'

'Stephen Myers.' The man had brought the camera back down, and was now walking away.

Emma made a move, but Dan gripped her arm. 'Emma, he's *dead*. Stephen Myers is gone.'

She continued watching the man. 'I know, but . . .'

'Em, please, it's just your mind playing tricks on you.' Dan's voice was full of worry – he had turned and was scanning the street where Emma was looking, but couldn't see anyone who looked even remotely suspicious. 'After everything that's happened, it's perfectly natural.'

'Come with me,' she said. 'Come and see for certain.'

Dan hesitated. Just long enough for Emma to set off ahead of him.

She jogged at a relaxed pace, but one that would close the gap between herself and the man within a minute.

Dan ran up alongside her. 'Em, this is crazy!'

'I know,' she said, 'but I need to see for certain.'

They were closing in on him, dodging the tourists as they went. The man, who was walking casually, turned down a side road. Emma wasn't sure whether he might have seen them with a snatched sideways glance. Again, she couldn't see his face properly. But the hair colour and body shape – it *could* be him . . .

Emma picked up the pace. She didn't want to lose him. Dan kept up, with no attempt to hold her back or convince her to stop the pursuit. They ran across the road, skirting around the back of a delivery van that had just passed by.

But there was no sign of him in the side road – just a small group of elderly people who were milling around outside a café, perusing the menu. Emma came to a stop, frustrated. 'He must have hidden in one of the shops.' The side road was lined with shops of various kinds.

Dan placed a comforting hand on her upper arm. 'Em, he's *dead*.'

Emma nodded, realising with a sudden awakening that she was behaving irrationally. 'I know he's dead. I know it's all in my mind. But it doesn't make it feel any less real.'

Dan pulled her towards him. 'I know it doesn't.'

Lizzy got through the matinée without any slip-ups. It wasn't her best performance by any means but, under the circumstances, she thought she had done pretty well. There were no fluffed lines. And her singing voice had remained strong throughout. Her tactic had been to push the words of Adrian Spencer as far towards the back of her mind as possible. And in truth, during the show, she had only thought about them briefly.

But now, back in the dressing room, they were up front and centre.

For the past month she had been trying to ignore the situation, but now that he knew, she had to take another path.

It was time to talk to Will.

8

Emma and Dan's first morning in St Ives was fantastic, as she put the scare of earlier behind her. First they went for tea and scones at The Tea Room, one of St Ives' highly recommended tea shops, and talked things through: it was about accepting that what she was going through, what they were all going through, was a perfectly natural reaction to the extremely stressful experience that was, after all, still fresh in their minds. By the time they had finished, Emma felt a lot better.

After that they strolled along the seafront, taking in the sights of the fishing boats in the harbour and holiday-makers spread out over the beach, enjoying the sunshine. It might have been October, but with the unseasonably mild weather, St Ives was buzzing with people. Children splashed in the clear, blue waters, and around the headland an army of black-suited surfers rode the waves, flipping off and onto their boards in their quest for the perfect ride.

At lunchtime, having explored all the shops on the high street, they bought some fish and chips and sat on the sea wall, just in front of the Tate art gallery.

'I couldn't be happier,' Emma said, popping a chip into her mouth and resting her shoulder against Dan's. 'Thanks for calming me down earlier. I feel so much better now.'

Dan put his arm around her back and held her close. He looked off into the distance, far out to sea, as if searching for the right words. Emma watched his face. He looked troubled. 'Me, too,' he said finally.

'Are you okay?'

He nodded unconvincingly. 'You know, there was a time when I thought I'd never see you again.' He traced his tongue along his top lip, and Emma knew that meant he was struggling to contain his emotions.

She squeezed his hand. 'It's okay – we *should* talk about this now. I know what we said back in the apartment, about forgetting it all while we're away, but maybe this is the best place to deal with it. I mean, the way I reacted before, chasing after that man, thinking he was, well, you know. It just shows that we can't ignore things. We can't run from it.'

There was a tear glinting in the corner of Dan's eye. 'I was so scared, Em.' He shook his head. 'I've never been as scared in my life.'

'Scared of Peter Myers?'

'No, scared of losing you.'

She nodded, slowly. 'I was afraid of losing you, too,' she replied. 'There were points when I thought you might already be . . .'

'Dead?'

Emma couldn't bring herself to say the word.

'Is that why—?' Dan stopped himself, looking out again towards open water.

'What?'

'Oh, I don't know,' he said, blowing out a gust of air.

She made him look her in the eyes. 'No, Dan, don't keep things bottled up. You've got to let these things out.'

He gathered himself. 'Is that why you got close to Stuart Harris again?'

Emma hadn't been expecting that. She didn't know what to say. 'I . . .'

Dan swallowed. 'I saw the photographs on the *Daily Post* website. You were on that boat with him, sailing down the Thames, drinking champagne.'

Immediately, Emma felt on the defensive. The Thames cruise seemed like a lifetime ago, but here it was, causing trouble. It wasn't really surprising that Dan had found the photographs

– the event had been covered extensively by the tabloids, as well as several other media outlets. She had seen the pictures herself, and worried about what Dan might think if he ever came across them – she had hoped that in the aftermath of his rescue they would remain undiscovered.

Maybe I should have come clean in the first place.

'I was invited at short notice, by Guy Roberts. It was to publicise the movie – the whole cast and crew were on board. But I swear, I didn't know that Stuart would be there. It wasn't planned, I promise.'

'But you *were* drinking champagne with him.'

'I had some champagne and got chatting to him. We went out onto the deck, watching the sights go by, but there was nothing more to it. It wasn't like it looks from those photographs.'

'I know,' Dan said sadly, looking as though he regretted that it had happened at all. 'I know it wasn't. I didn't mean it like that.'

Emma searched for the words. She didn't feel angry at what Dan had suggested; she felt guilty. She had, for however short a period, got too close to Stuart Harris. Yes, he had used her, but she had been somewhat willing. And then the moment had come when he had tried to kiss her, and she had suddenly realised the reality of what was happening.

Is this *why Dan has been acting so strangely since his release?* Had it not been about his incarceration at all? Had it been about *them*? If so, then for the good of their relationship, it needed dealing with now.

'I love *you*, Dan, not Stuart. Please believe me. I did love him, a long time ago, but honestly, he wasn't half the man you are. And the way I feel about you, well, it's totally different to anything I've ever felt before. It's on another level – always has been, always will be.'

Dan nodded. 'I'm sorry, Em. I shouldn't have questioned you like that. I do trust you, totally. It's just that when I saw those photos you looked so . . . happy.'

Emma wanted to cry. She could empathise totally with how he must have felt seeing those images, taken at the time when he'd been imprisoned, with the world not knowing whether he was dead or alive. 'Maybe in that moment,' she admitted. 'But you know what photos are like – sometimes they don't tell the real story. I wasn't *really* happy. How could I be? My fiancé was missing. I wish I'd never gone to that event, but I guess it was just how I got through it all – Peter Myers making me think that you'd left me, sending those weird text messages, pretending to be you . . . it was all meant to make me believe that you didn't want to be with me any more.'

'I'm being an idiot,' Dan said, nodding. 'We were having a lovely time, trying to get over things, and I'm going on like this, jealous about someone who isn't even alive any more.'

'You're not an idiot.' Emma squeezed his hand. 'You're just being honest about how you feel. There's nothing wrong with that. It would be wrong to say nothing, and go on worrying. That's not a good way to start a marriage.'

'You still want to get married?'

'Of course I do!'

'Even though I doubted you?'

'Come on,' Emma said, getting up and pulling Dan to his feet. 'I'll race you to the sea. Last one there has to sit with my mad Aunty Ruth at the wedding reception.'

They sprinted off, laughing, towards the water's edge, completely unaware that they were being watched.

They spent a good hour walking barefoot by the sea, carrying their shoes, letting the warm waves lap over their feet. It was so relaxing, and felt a world away from the hustle and bustle of London.

'I *am* sorry,' Dan said, turning to face Emma and taking both her hands in his. 'I feel terrible for questioning you about Stuart. I do trust you. But I've been feeling so afraid that you might have changed your mind about how you feel about me. I guess this whole experience has shaken me up more than I thought, and it's made me question things that I've always taken for granted. It feels like the ground has shifted – like an earthquake, and it still hasn't quite settled. Do you understand?'

Emma nodded. She knew exactly what he meant, and in fact it was a huge relief to find out that she wasn't the only one who felt as if the world had been destabilised. 'Like aftershocks.'

'Yes,' he said. 'That's it, exactly – aftershocks. Just when I think I'm okay, another one comes along and knocks me sideways. I realise then that everything isn't quite back to normal.'

'I know just what you mean.'

Then she summoned the courage to ask the question she'd been desperate to ask for the past hour: 'The reason you didn't want to go ahead and re-arrange the wedding too soon – was it because you felt unsure about how I felt about Stuart?'

Dan pressed his toes into the wet sand. 'Partly . . . I'm sorry, Em.'

'It's okay, I understand. I appreciate your honesty.'

'I should have spoken to you about it sooner. But it never really felt like the right time. And I didn't intend to tell you here, on holiday, either, but it just came out.'

'Well, I'm glad that it did. Because now we've been able to deal with it.'

Dan nodded. They looked at each other for a few moments, and then kissed, holding the moment even as three children splashed past them, shouting with delight. 'I do love you, Emma Holden.'

Emma looked into his eyes. 'I love you, too.'

They kissed again, and held each other close. Emma could feel the comforting sound of Dan's heart beating.

'I've got a surprise for you,' Dan said. 'You remember you mentioned the open-air theatre, carved into the cliff-side?'

'The Minack Theatre, yes.'

'That's it. Well, they're currently running a production of *Romeo and Juliet*, and I've got us tickets for this evening!'

'Oh, wow! My favourite play!'

'I know.' Dan smiled. 'I do listen to what you say, you know. Well, most of the time, anyway.'

'Thanks, it's going to be great.' Emma had played Juliet in a school play, many years ago. The fact that it had been such an unforgettable experience was one of the reasons she had decided to go into acting, so it held a special place in her heart. She kissed Dan again. 'Thanks so much.'

They walked back across the beach, as the man who Emma had chased down the street fired off another round of snaps.

9

'Are you okay?'

Amy put a hand on Will's arm as he looked up at the London Eye from the relative comfort of the queue.

The thing is just so high.

'Yeah, I'm fine,' Will lied, with a forced smile. He went to bite a cuticle on his fingernail, but stopped himself as he didn't want to reveal his true nerves.

Amy didn't look convinced. 'It will be fine, I promise. But if you don't want to do it, then that's *absolutely* okay. The worst thing would be to force you to do something like this. I'd totally understand. You've already conquered one fear for today, so that's pretty good going.'

Will smiled, properly this time. Yes, he had conquered a fear. And a very ingrained one at that – just as ingrained as his fear of heights. He looked up again at the wheel. 'I can do this,' he said. 'It might be a bit painful, but I can do it.'

That earned him a kiss on the cheek. 'That's the spirit, Will Holden.'

The queue moved forward quickly and, before he knew it, they were standing at the front of it. The steward gestured for them to step forward and, as they entered the pod, Will was heady with nerves.

The pod, its curved outer shell see-through on all sides, was just a few metres square. Inside it, just over twenty people fitted, either standing around the edges or sitting in a bench-like structure in its centre. Will headed straight for the bench, and planted himself down. Two small children brushed past his knees as they ran for the front, their parents close behind. 'Sophie, Toby, careful!'

Amy sat down next to Will. 'We can sit here – that's fine. Then maybe you might feel like standing later.'

Will looked outside. The pod was already climbing, but slowly – the pods didn't in fact stop: the wheel went slowly enough so that people could embark and disembark as it moved. 'How long does this last again?'

'About thirty minutes.'

It will be a long half an hour ...

But with the twenty or so people around him, Will could almost forget where he was. Ten minutes in, his head tilted low, all he could really see was shoes. He certainly couldn't see anything outside the pod. With his vision restricted, he calmed down. But he knew that just getting through it wasn't the point of the exercise. It was cheating. He turned to Amy, who had stayed loyally alongside him. She smiled supportively.

She must be bored stiff, not being able to see out properly.

Will nodded. 'Let's stand up.'

Amy smiled again. She took his hand as they got to their feet. Immediately, Will regretted his decision – the pod was much higher than he had imagined, and he could see far down to the Thames at the tiny boats below. London spread out far and wide, like a model city, bathed in sunshine. He stiffened, gripping Amy's hand tightly as he peered down at the floor. 'Sorry,' he managed to say, loosening his hold against all his natural instincts.

'It's fine,' she said, even though the grip must have hurt. 'Do you want to sit back down?'

He swallowed his fears. 'No. I'll be okay.' He forced himself to look outside again. It didn't feel quite as scary this time. And then he looked around the pod. There were people of all ages – the two youngsters who had rushed past him were pressing their hands against the outer shell; an elderly couple was gazing out towards the far horizon; and a group of teenagers was chatting and laughing. No one seemed anxious.

'Would you like to move closer to the edge?' Amy ventured. 'It would be a pity to waste a good view.'

Will wasn't sure if he would be able to do it but, emboldened by how far he had come that day, he felt an irresistible urge to try. 'Okay.'

Taking tiny steps, he moved gingerly past people until he was at the edge of the pod. Down below to their left was the Palace of Westminster, the seat of government. Holding his breath, and with sweaty palms, he gazed down on Westminster Bridge, tracking a London bus as it traversed the river. Below it, a tourist cruiser glided past along the shimmering waters.

'How do you feel?' Amy asked at his shoulder.

'Okay,' Will said. And he meant it. He was feeling fine – surprisingly calm, considering his long-standing problem. 'Look,' he said, 'you can see over to where Emma and Dan live.' He pointed towards the area east of the BT Tower. Further than that, he thought he could see the green expanse of Regent's Park, where they had met that morning.

'I just love the bird's-eye view you get,' Amy said. 'I love to look down and see things from above.'

'Is that why you skydive?'

'One of the reasons, yes. I love the feeling of falling too, when you jump out of the plane, the exhilaration of . . .' She stopped, realising that talking about falling was not going to help Will just then. 'But, yes, looking down from above, there's just something so amazing about it.'

Will continued to take in the view. 'I can see that. I know now what I've been missing out on.'

'I'm impressed,' Amy said. 'Do you realise we're at the highest point now?'

Will looked to one side and could see the next pod, slightly below them – off to the other side it was the same. They were at the top of the wheel. 'That feels a bit funny,' he admitted, his balance wobbling slightly.

'We'll be on our way back down in a minute.'

'I'm okay,' Will said, looking again at the next-door pod. He was amazed to see that the couple inside it had it all to themselves, as they leant against the barrier at the front, sipping champagne.

'Wow,' said Amy, as she looked over to where he was staring. 'You know, I'd heard that you could do that. I'd love to drink champagne when I'm looking at this view. Costs a lot though.'

'Maybe next time,' Will joked.

Fifteen minutes later they disembarked and moved away, down the ramp, hand in hand.

'That was *fantastic*,' Will said. He turned and looked back up at the structure. 'I can't believe I did it. I mean, when I think back to the time that the others went on it, and I stayed on the ground. It just felt so miserable. And now I've done it!'

'Another fear slain,' Amy said. 'You've done well today.'

Will grinned. 'I have, haven't I?'

Will took a beer out of the fridge, flicked on the television and flopped down onto the sofa. He was on a high. What a fabulous day. And Amy was such an amazing girl. In many ways, the trip on the London Eye had been just as terrifying as the encounter with the spider, but, likewise, to take on and conquer his fear of heights was equally fantastic. Again, Amy had been the spur, challenging him to do things he had shied away from all his life. He'd never met anyone like her before. Least of all, someone like her who seemed to like him – he'd never had the best luck in the romance department.

Will she stick around?

He took a swig from the bottle and channel-hopped. He could see himself marrying her, although it was, of course, very early days, and there was no way on earth that he would admit such a thing to Amy. Surely something like that would send her running for the hills. He didn't even know if she agreed with marriage, or wanted children, or—

Stop it.

But why not wallow in the joy of the moment? After all, it might be the real deal. And if it wasn't, then it was still better to enjoy it while it lasted. Amy's life philosophy was definitely rubbing off on him. To think he used to be such a pessimistic idiot.

The door buzzer sounded at ten past seven, just as he was preparing a microwave pasta meal. It was Lizzy. She looked flustered – definitely not her usual self.

'Hi, Lizzy,' he said, as she entered the flat. 'You okay?'

'I need to ask you something.' She took a seat and avoided the pleasantries. 'It's going to sound weird, I know it is, but I just need to ask you.'

Will sat down opposite her. It already sounded weird. And she looked spooked. It brought back bad memories of those awful couple of weeks, just one short month ago. 'What's the matter?'

Lizzy gathered her thoughts. 'That reporter from the *Daily Post*, Adrian Spencer . . . has he spoken to you today?'

'No. Not since I told him to get lost. That was, what, maybe three days ago, the last time he phoned me. Has he been bothering you again?'

'He followed me onto the bus this morning.'

Will was aghast. 'What? That's terrible – he's *stalking* you. He's really stepped over the line. I hope you told him where to go.'

'I did. But then he told me something.'

Will didn't like the sound of this. 'Go on.'

She cleared her throat. 'I don't quite know how to say this,' she began. 'Er . . . well, when you . . .'

'Lizzy, you're really worrying me.'

'He's spoken to Peter Myers,' she blurted out. 'In the past week – to gather information for the article.'

Suddenly Will knew what this was all about, and his stomach knotted. He could hardly get the words out. 'Did he tell him about . . . what I did? Helping Stuart to get rid of Stephen's body?'

They had all wondered why Peter Myers had not told the police about Will's involvement in his son's death. One theory was that he was just waiting for the right time. Another, that for as long as he held on to the secret, he felt he would still have some power over them.

Will had never really doubted that one day he would have to answer to the police for what he had done.

But why now, *when things are going so well?*

'It's not that,' Lizzy said. 'I don't think he knows anything like that about what happened.'

Will was hugely relieved. 'Then what is it about?'

Again Lizzy paused ominously, extinguishing his relief. 'All those years ago, when Stuart called you round to his flat, after he'd killed Stephen Myers, did you see his body?'

Will was taken aback by the question. 'Well, yes, of course I did. You know I helped to get rid of . . . it. You know that.'

'Sorry, Will, I understand that. What I meant was, did you see his *face* – are you sure it was him – his body?'

Again Will was dumbstruck. 'What's this all about, Lizzy?'

Lizzy seemed exasperated. 'Just answer me, Will. Did you see his face?'

The images of that fateful day rose from the gloom. 'No. Not properly. I couldn't bring myself to look at him. Stuart dealt with it mostly, and I helped to carry him once he was wrapped up in the bed sheets. By then he was covered.'

This didn't seem to be the answer Lizzy had wanted to hear. 'But what about when you got to the canal? You removed him from the sheets then, didn't you?'

'Yes, but again, I didn't look directly at him. I saw his body, yes, but not his face. It was him, though. It was Stephen Myers.'

'How can you be so sure?'

'Because the police would have checked that, wouldn't they? And his family – he would have been identified by them.'

'But they said that his body had decomposed, and had been attacked by animals. It had been in the water for days. Maybe they just assumed—'

'Why would you think it might not have been him?'

Lizzy swallowed and looked Will straight in the eyes. Again there was that haunted expression. 'I should have told you all before now. But I didn't know what to do – I didn't want to upset things, so I kept it secret . . .'

'It's okay, Lizzy, just tell me.'

Lizzy nodded. 'When I was being held by Peter Myers, just after he'd taken me . . . he told me that Stephen is still alive.'

10

The Minack Theatre was, according to the satnav, about half an hour's drive round the coast from Dan and Emma's holiday apartment. But, underestimating the time it would take to negotiate the unfamiliar, twisting Cornish roads and steep, narrow lanes, they arrived later than planned, just ten minutes before the performance was due to begin. The cliff-top car park was already nearly full, and they were lucky to squeeze into a small space between two poorly parked four-wheel drives.

'Amazing view,' Emma said, as they queued to enter the theatre. Off towards the left were magnificent, sheer-face cliffs that dropped down towards a long, sandy beach. The light was fading, casting shadows across the cliff-face, which made the sight even more spectacular.

Dan looked across towards them. 'From what I've read, I think it's even better from inside the theatre itself.'

He was right. The theatre, and the view it afforded, were amazing. Nestling into the partly excavated cliff, the theatre made the most of what nature offered. There were no chairs; instead, the audience perched on stone terracing in an amphitheatre design, interspersed with beautiful floral displays. In front of them the sea spread out like a huge canvas, framing the small stage at the edge of the cliff-side in darkening blue.

Most of the audience had already taken their seats, and there weren't any spaces below halfway to the front. Emma took her seat alongside Dan towards the back of the amphitheatre, on the left-hand side, squeezing in between two other couples. She looked across at the view. 'Wow. It would be so amazing to perform here. And it would make a fantastic wedding venue, too.'

'Seriously, you'd like to get married here?'

'Yeah, why not – can you imagine how spectacular the wedding photos would be, with that backdrop?'

Dan nodded in agreement.

A few minutes later the play began. As night descended, the atmosphere deepened to even greater levels. It was certainly the most stunning arena Emma had ever seen. She thought again about the idea of moving down to Cornwall. Maybe it wasn't such a crazy notion after all – the way she felt at that moment, she could happily work on this stage for the rest of her days. Who needed the West End when you could perform in such an amazing natural setting?

It was just after the interval that Emma noticed the man looking back up towards where they were sitting. It was impossible to see his face properly, because he was some way down the terracing and it was too dark but, without doubt, every so often he would turn round and look towards where Emma and Dan were. The first few times she had noticed him, he seemed to be scanning the audience but, later, he appeared to have found what he was searching for, as his eyes stayed fixed in their direction. Of course he couldn't have been looking at them, she knew that really, but it certainly seemed like it. She found her attention drifting away from the play as she began to check periodically to see what the man was doing. Mostly he was facing forwards, towards the stage, but sometimes he *was* looking back. It was beginning to freak her out.

She didn't want to speak during the performance – it was a pet hate of all actors – so she resisted saying anything to Dan, who seemed engrossed in the play. Instead, she pulled her jacket tightly around her, as the temperature dropped and an increasingly chilly sea wind whirled around them. Dan did notice that movement, and responded by wrapping his arm around her.

Emma soon forgot about the man and began to lose herself once more in the action onstage; by the time the play finished, she had forgotten all about him. The audience stood as one to applaud the cast; it had been impressive, and the standing ovation was well deserved. The lights came on and everyone began their slow progress towards the exit at the top of the amphitheatre.

'I'm just nipping to the toilet,' Emma said, as they neared the exits.

'Me, too,' Dan replied. 'See you over there.' He gestured towards the small shop, off to their right.

Emma nodded and headed towards the nearby toilets. There was a long queue. At first she decided to stay and joined the dozens of people standing outside the door. But after a few minutes without movement, she began to get impatient and wondered whether there were any other facilities. She looked around and saw an usher, who was standing guard by one of the railings.

'Excuse me, are there any other toilets apart from the ones over there? The queue's really long.'

'There aren't any more public toilets,' said the woman, slightly hesitantly, 'but sometimes we let people use the staff facilities. It should be okay. They're just over there.' She pointed to the far right-hand side of the arena. 'They're not signed as toilets. There are only two cubicles, but it should be quieter. Just go through the blue door.'

'Thanks.'

The staff toilets were down in a quiet corner of the theatre, already empty of people. Emma felt slightly guilty when she saw there was no queue and that she could just walk straight in. But she felt better that others had asked too, as, whilst she was in the cubicle, she heard the outer door open and close.

Now someone else was present she felt slightly unnerved, and wanted to return to the crowds, where Dan would already be waiting.

She was just about to leave the cubicle when the toes of a pair of brown, scuffed shoes appeared underneath the door. She stifled a scream.

He wore shoes like that!

What on earth?

She froze, afraid to move or even breathe. There was a man standing right outside the cubicle, so close to the door that his shoes were peeking underneath.

Then she realised – the staff toilets were probably unisex. As the woman had said, there was no sign on the door, nothing to indicate men or women, so that was probably the case.

And the shoes must be a coincidence.

But still, why was the person standing right outside? The cubicle next door was free. And if you were waiting, who would stand so close? It certainly wasn't socially acceptable behaviour.

She stared at the shoes, willing the person to leave, wondering whether she should say something.

The person stayed rooted to the spot and Emma's heart rate quickened.

Maybe one of the workers saw me enter the toilets, and is waiting to tell me off for using staff facilities?

'The lady said it was okay for me to come in here,' Emma said, her voice full of nerves. 'The other toilets were busy, so she said it was okay to use these.'

No response came. The shoes didn't even move a millimetre. Emma regretted opening her mouth. What if it wasn't a member of staff? She had just given away the fact that she was a woman.

Then she remembered the man in the audience.

'Please, go,' she mouthed silently. 'Please.'

What if he *had* been watching her? What if he'd followed her out towards the top of the theatre, then to the public toilets, and now to the staff facilities?

The thought seemed ludicrous – there was no reason to believe he had even been looking at her. But here she was, trapped in this cubicle, with an unidentified man just inches away.

She pulled her mobile phone out of her pocket, and then summoned up the courage to speak again. This time she suppressed her nerves, holding her voice steady. 'If you don't leave, right now, I'm going to call my boyfriend. He'll be down here in seconds.'

Still no movement.

'I'm dialling then,' she said.

Dan picked up on the third ring. 'Hi, Em.'

'Dan, I'm in the staff toilets, on the right-hand side of the theatre. Can you get here, right now? It's the unmarked blue door.'

'Are you okay? You sound—'

'Some guy is standing right outside my cubicle.'

A split-second hesitation, then: 'I'll be there right away.'

The shoes disappeared and Emma heard the outer door open and close.

'Thank God.'

Dan arrived just twenty or so seconds later. 'Em, are you in there? It's okay, it's me.'

She opened the door and they hugged. She could feel her heart beating hard against Dan's chest. 'Did you see the person coming out of the toilets?'

'No. I didn't see anyone.'

They reported the incident at the office. The staff took it extremely seriously and even offered to call the police, but there seemed little point. What could they do? There was some CCTV on site, but none covering that area, so it would have been impossible to identify the person. And although it had been a scary, intimidating experience, no crime had been committed. The toilets were indeed unisex, so the man, whoever he was, had had every right to be there.

'Are you okay?' Dan said, back in the car, as they fastened their seat belts and prepared to leave.

'I'm fine.'

He looked across at her. 'You still look shaken.'

'It's okay. It just really reminded me of all those bad things from the past – Stephen Myers, Peter Myers, you know, being stalked. I never want to go back to that – *never*.'

Dan nodded. 'You won't have to go back. I won't let it happen.'

Emma reached for his hand. 'I know you won't. I just, well, I just don't understand what happened there.'

Dan shrugged. 'Just someone playing a sick joke maybe. Getting a kick out of scaring strangers.'

'Maybe.'

'You think something different?'

Now it was Emma's turn to shrug. She thought back to the man in the audience. 'You're probably right. I was just in the wrong place at the wrong time.'

'C'mon,' said Dan, still looking at her. 'Let's go. We'll get back to the apartment, chill out for a while and put this behind us. I'm really sorry this happened, Em. It was supposed to be such a good night.'

They reached the apartment complex just before ten o'clock. Emma was still shaken, but on the journey back the memory had already begun to fade a little. She'd convinced herself that there couldn't have been a connection between the man in the audience and the person in the toilets. She had been a random, rather than targeted, victim.

It was the only explanation that seemed plausible.

They used their key-card at the main entrance, climbed the stairs and turned left towards their apartment door. Outside, on the mat, was a large bouquet of assorted flowers – reds, blues, purples, yellows.

Emma smiled and turned to Dan.

But he didn't smile back. 'They're not from me, sorry.'

Emma frowned and picked up the bouquet. Something was wrong with this. She found the note at the back of the flowers – a single, terrifying sentence.

I'm still your number one fan.

Part Two

11

'What do you want me to do with these?' Dan asked, as he stood in the centre of the room, the bouquet hanging at his side.

Emma looked up from the sofa, where she had been sitting, her head in her hands. After reading the note she'd come running in and drawn all the curtains, as if that might shut out the unseen danger that lurked outside.

This couldn't be happening.

The phrase, *I'm your number one fan* – it was Stephen Myers, all over again. The first time Emma had heard him utter that was when he had approached her outside the television studios. He would go on to say it many times after, and Emma had never doubted that he believed what he said. He truly thought that it was a positive statement, when in fact it filled Emma with horror.

'Have you locked the door?' she asked.

'Yes. I slid the chain across, too. No one can get in.'

Emma shuddered at the thought. Sure, the door was locked, but the thought that someone knew where they were staying, and had arranged for those flowers to be delivered, with *that* message . . .? It was just scary. And after what had happened at the theatre.

'Shall I put the flowers back outside?' he said.

Emma nodded. 'If you don't mind. I can't bear to look at them.'

Dan did as requested and returned a few seconds later. 'Everything's locked up again. There's no need to—' He stopped himself, realising that what he was about to say was stupid. 'Of course, it's worrying.' He ran a hand through his hair.

'Whoever did this, they know where we're staying,' Emma said.

'I know,' he said gravely. 'Do you want to leave?'

'What? Go and stay somewhere else?'

'Yes. If you're not comfortable staying here, then let's go somewhere else.'

Emma thought it over. 'It's holiday season. It might be difficult to find somewhere, this late at night.'

'Possibly.'

'Plus, I don't really want to go outside again tonight. Not knowing that someone might be out there.'

Dan came and sat down beside Emma, putting an arm around her. 'I totally understand.' He dropped his head back onto the sofa back, so that he was peering up at the ceiling. He exhaled. 'Em,' he said, bringing his head back down. 'Whoever sent those, they do know where we're staying, but it doesn't mean that they're here.'

'What do you mean?'

'Well, they could have called the florists, and asked them to deliver the flowers. They could have done that from London, or anywhere.'

'Maybe.'

'You don't think so?'

'What about the person at the theatre?' she said. 'It's connected, Dan, I'm sure it is. And the person I saw in town today. Maybe I wasn't just imagining things.'

'You really think this could be Stephen Myers?'

'I know it sounds ridiculous . . .'

'It doesn't matter if it sounds ridiculous or not,' Dan said. 'What matters is how you feel about it.'

Emma ran a hand across her face. 'There's something else I didn't tell you.'

'Go on.'

'At the theatre. I thought a man near the front of the auditorium was looking at us.'

'What? During the performance?'

'Yes. I didn't say anything because I wasn't sure. But after what happened afterwards, I'm beginning to wonder—'

'Whether it's all the same person,' Dan finished.

Emma closed her eyes.

Dan drew her closer. 'Shall we call the police?'

'Maybe in the morning. Let's just go to bed. I feel exhausted.' Emma looked across at the table, where she had placed the card that had accompanied the flowers. She had a thought. 'The name of the florists is on the card. I wonder if it's local.' She reached across and read the text, trying to avoid looking at the creepy message. 'Bella's Bouquets.'

Dan checked, using his phone. 'It's only just down the road.' He showed her the screen. 'It's on the main road, just before Tesco.'

Emma nodded. They must have passed the florists on the road that snaked around the coast towards St Ives when they had gone to the supermarket to stock up with essentials on their arrival. 'We can go there tomorrow.'

'And they'll be able to confirm who bought the flowers.'

'Hopefully.'

'Tomorrow it is then.'

'Morning,' Dan said, as Emma entered the living area at nine o'clock the next morning. 'I've got breakfast ready.'

Fresh coffee and croissants were producing a mouth-watering aroma. Dan was sitting in front of the laptop they had brought with them, knowing that the apartment had Wi-Fi. 'I found out the opening times,' he said, chewing on one of the pastries. 'It'll be open in the next hour.' He sounded business-like, in control, which was reassuring.

Emma joined him on the sofa, tucking her legs underneath her body. She yawned.

Dan turned to her. 'You didn't sleep well again, did you?'

'I think I must have woken up virtually every hour,' she replied. 'I kept thinking I could hear something, or someone, outside.' She still felt incredibly shaken after last night's incidents.

'You should have woken me up,' Dan said. 'I was dead to the world.'

'There's no point you being shattered, too.'

Dan pointed at the onscreen map, showing the route from their apartment complex to the florists. 'It's quick to walk. It'll only take a few minutes.'

She glanced at the clock on the wall. 'Just time for breakfast and a shower. We can be there for when it opens.'

'Are you sure about this?'

'Definitely – if there's a chance of finding out who sent those flowers, I want to know. I'm tired of running away from these kinds of people.'

'And what about the police?'

'Let's see what the florist says first.'

'Can I help you?'

The woman behind the counter laid down a bunch of flowers that she was preparing, and took off her glasses.

Emma prayed that she'd be receptive and helpful. 'I received a bouquet of flowers last night, from your shop, and I wondered if you could tell me who sent them.'

The woman blinked at them for a second or two. 'We don't usually give out names. If the sender doesn't request it to be on a card, then we assume they may want to remain anonymous.'

This hadn't started well. Emma tried a different tactic. 'The message on the card, it was threatening.'

The woman looked confused. 'Threatening? We wouldn't allow something threatening to be sent—'

'It might not have seemed threatening to you. But it has a specific meaning for me.'

'Right,' the woman said, drawing out the 'i' sound. She put her glasses back on and opened a large book on the counter, beginning to leaf through it. 'May I ask your name, please?'

'Emma. Emma Holden.'

The woman traced down the page with her finger. 'Emma Holden. You're staying at the Sunset View apartments. "I'm still your number one fan"?'

'I was stalked once by someone who used to say he was my number one fan,' Emma explained.

The lady looked troubled. 'I see. And you think this is from him?'

'No. He's dead.'

'Oh, right. Well, how—?'

'It's someone who knows about what happened, and is doing this to try and frighten me. I think they followed us last night, when we went to the Minack Theatre, as they arranged for the flowers to be delivered for when we got back. That's why we need to know who it is.'

Emma wasn't totally convinced that the person who had sent the flowers was also the individual from the theatre toilets, but it was certainly a possibility, and she thought linking the two now would strengthen her case for being given the name.

The lady pursed her lips. 'Don't you need to speak to the police about this?'

'We already did,' Dan said. 'Last night. They're not interested.'

Emma was surprised by the speed and ease with which Dan lied. They hadn't yet called the police, deciding that it would probably be better to contact Detective Inspector Gasnier when they returned home. The local police wouldn't understand the background to it all, and would surely only be able to offer general advice about minimising risks in the event that this really was something sinister. But the reality was that nothing concrete had happened. And without the police really understanding the context of their concerns, it would be natural for their reaction to be lukewarm.

The lady seemed convinced. She looked at Dan, then at Emma, and back down at her book, tapping the page. 'Okay,' she said. 'Okay, I'll tell you. As I said, we don't normally disclose names, but I think on this occasion, I'll make an exception.'

'Thank you,' Emma said, relieved and grateful. 'It means a lot.'

The lady raised her eyes from the book. 'Stephen Myers.'

Emma felt a blast of sickness slam into her. 'The person said they were called Stephen Myers?'

'Yes,' the woman said, matter-of-factly. 'It's written down here.'

'It's okay.' Dan placed a comforting hand on Emma's back.

'Are you all right?' the lady asked. 'Does that name mean anything to you?'

Emma nodded, fighting nausea. 'The person who ordered the flowers, did they do it by phone, or in person?'

'I'm not sure. I know I didn't serve them. But wait, it says here that they paid by cash, so it couldn't have been over the telephone. Hang on one moment.' She turned towards an open door behind her. 'Alice, can you come here for a second?'

An attractive girl in her late teens appeared, wearing green gloves and a pretty, flowery apron. She smiled at Dan and Emma.

'Alice, did you serve this gentleman?' The lady pointed to the book.

The girl nodded. 'He came in yesterday, early morning.'

'Can you describe him?' Emma asked.

'He was about your height,' said Alice, nodding towards Dan, 'but very thin. His face was thin too, you know, hollow-looking. His nose was quite, well, prominent, pointy. Sorry,' she added, suddenly looking embarrassed, 'is he a friend of yours?'

'No.' Emma's heart was racing. This girl was describing Stephen Myers, or at least how Emma remembered him. 'What colour hair did he have?'

'It was dark. Dark brown, I think, not black.'

That was right, too. But it *couldn't* be. He was dead, buried six feet under in the churchyard that Peter Myers had taken them to.

To think otherwise was ludicrous.

'Eye colour?'

'Sorry, I didn't notice that.'

And then the question Emma felt was almost too crazy to ask: 'Did you notice anything else about him, anything about his face?'

Would she mention the scarring?

'Well, yes,' the girl said, slowly. 'His face was quite, well, acne-scarred. The top of his cheeks, in particular. Sorry, that sounds really rude of me. I'm not meaning to criticise the guy. He seemed nice and friendly.'

'It can't be,' Emma said, closing her eyes, as the room started spinning around her. 'It's not possible.'

12

Edward finished a light breakfast of toast and jam and retreated back to his study with a cup of tea, while Miranda took a shower. He hadn't felt like eating, and hadn't slept well that night. In the early hours he had slunk out of bed without waking Miranda, and gone downstairs to read the rest of Saturday's newspaper in the kitchen. There, in the half-light, he had skimmed the pages, but for the most part his mind had been elsewhere.

Now he slipped down into his leather chair, picked up a biro that lay on the desk and tapped it rhythmically against the wood surface.

What have I done?

It hadn't gone how he had planned: the questions that the man had asked; the way he had asked them. It had felt more like a witch hunt than anything else. Just a few minutes into their conversation, Edward had known that he had made a terrible mistake. Believing that he could not only limit, but reverse the damage he was causing, he had continued on, trying desperately to reframe the debate. But that had been delusional. He had had no chance of being in control – they were too good for that. Too driven.

He traced his tongue around his lips, thinking.

Another few taps of the pen. Then a glance at the wall clock.

He should be up by now, even on a Sunday.

He called the number and waited fearfully. Finally the man picked up, with a curt 'Yes?'

'It's Edward Holden. Listen, I've been thinking, and I've changed my mind. I'd like you to discount what was said yesterday, wipe it from the record . . . Yes, but surely, if I've changed my mind then ... Well, that's just ... You wouldn't dare! ... Please, I'm begging you ...' He couldn't believe what he was hearing. And just when he thought that things couldn't get any worse – 'Hello? Hello?'

He'd cut the call.

Edward held the phone next to his ear, frozen in disbelief and dread. It was too late. He'd made his choice, and now there was no going back.

'What do you want to do?' Dan asked, as they made their way back down the road towards the apartment complex.

Emma paused at the zebra crossing and the traffic stopped to let them cross. 'I don't want to run away, and spoil our holiday,' she said, as they thanked the drivers while crossing.

'But it's already been spoilt, hasn't it?'

Emma nodded, and stopped, putting a hand to her head. 'You've spent so much money, on such a fantastic apartment.'

'I know, but that's not important, is it? Money doesn't matter, compared to our safety.'

Emma shook her head in disbelief at the situation. 'What's going on, Dan?'

'I don't know – I really don't.'

They continued walking.

'Are you all right, Em?'

She shrugged. 'I'm still trying to get my head around this. Someone is stalking me again, pretending to be Stephen Myers.'

'So you don't think any more that it is actually him?'

Emma stopped again. 'Well, no ...' She searched for the words to explain. 'I mean, that's just ludicrous, isn't it? Stephen Myers is dead. I know what I said, about thinking that I saw him. But we know that isn't possible, don't we?'

Dan nodded.

'But I also know what I've seen – that time with Lizzy in the department store, at the service station, yesterday in St Ives and at the Minack last night. I mean, I was really starting to think that I was going crazy, as if I was just imaging it all. Now we know that I wasn't. Now we know that there is *someone* out there, wanting me to think that he is Stephen Myers. Who the hell would do something like that?'

Dan shrugged. 'Could be anyone, I guess. The story's been in all the papers.'

'Peter Myers is in jail,' Emma continued, 'so it can't be him. I mean, the person who ordered those flowers, he even looked like Stephen Myers.'

'I know.'

'And whoever this person is, they knew we were on holiday. They *knew* we were in Cornwall, they *knew* exactly where we are staying – the apartment number, everything. It makes me think that it might be someone close to me, for them to know so much detail about my life.'

Dan was dismissive. 'No one close to you would want to do that. I mean, who knows that we're down here? Will, Lizzy, your dad, Miranda.' He counted them off on his fingers. 'You don't think any of them would do this, do you?'

'No, of course not.'

'Did you tell anyone else?'

'No, no one else knows.' Emma thought for a few seconds. 'Do you think this person followed us from London?'

'Maybe – or it might have been a chance sighting. They might live down here, and have read about what happened in the news, and decided to play a sick joke on you.'

'I guess.' Emma thought about that scenario. It was actually the most appealing option, which was presumably why Dan had suggested it. 'Anything is better than the possibility of someone driving hundreds of miles, stalking us.' But then she thought back to what had happened en route to Cornwall, at the services. Unless she *had* just imagined the sighting, the person had been there then, which lent weight to the idea that they had been trailing her. 'Do you think what happened at the theatre is connected? The person in the toilets, do you think it is the same person who sent the flowers?'

'Well, I'd like to think not, but to be honest, yes.'

'Me, too.' She looked around. An old couple was walking up the opposite side of the road, holding hands. Coming towards them was a young family; the parents smiled a hello as the two children swung buckets and spades as they passed. And back at the top of the hill, vehicles sped past along the main road. There was no sign of a Stephen Myers impersonator. If this person was around, they couldn't be within earshot.

Dan noticed that Emma was distracted. 'But even if there isn't a connection between those two events, the reality is that someone who is around here sent those flowers to you, pretending to be Stephen Myers. And, like you said, they know exactly where we're staying. I think that we'd be mad to stick around here, don't you think?'

She turned her attention back to him. 'You're right.'

'Then it's settled – we'll go back and pack. If we stayed around for another two days and something happened, I'd never forgive myself.'

They agreed to get away as soon as possible, stacking everything in the hallway, just outside the apartment door. It didn't take long. After all, they had hardly had time to settle in, so most of their things were ready to take straight back out again.

'I know we agreed to leave as quickly as possible, but I just have to look at that view one more time before we go,' Emma said, moving over to the balcony. Dan followed, and they stood there, looking out at the wonderful vista in front of them. 'It's a real shame that we can't have more of this.'

'I know.' He put his arm around her. 'As soon as all this has settled down, we'll come back. I promise. Maybe in the spring, we'll come for a week, back to this same apartment if we can.'

'That would be amazing. But expensive.'

'Ah, don't worry about that,' he smiled. 'I've got a few months to start saving.' He pulled her closer and they spent a few more minutes looking out towards the open water and St Ives.

'You were pretty convincing back there,' Emma said eventually.

'What do you mean?'

'When you told the florist that we'd already spoken to the police.'

He shrugged it off, but released his hold slightly. 'A little white lie.'

'I don't think I've ever known you to lie.'

He laughed. 'Everybody lies, Em, if the situation calls for it. I'm not talking about big, fat lies. Don't you ever lie?'

'Yes, of course. You were just very convincing. If I hadn't known it was untrue, I would have believed you. I guess it was just a surprise that you were so polished.'

Now Dan looked slightly hurt. 'I don't make a habit of it. And I didn't really plan to say that. But I got the distinct impression that she wasn't going to tell us anything, not if she knew we hadn't been to the police. I just felt so strongly that we needed the name of the person who sent the flowers. So I thought if I said we had already contacted the police, it might convince her to talk.'

'Well, it certainly worked.'

'Yes. Yes, it did,' he said with finality. 'Now, c'mon, let's get going.'

Emma looked around longingly. 'Well, goodbye for now, beautiful apartment.'

'For now,' Dan emphasised. He strode over to the guest book and scribbled a message, along with the date and their names.

Emma took a look. The message read:

Amazing apartment, fantastic views. Will definitely be back very soon.

They hurried down to the car with their bags, slinging them into the vehicle as quickly as they could. There was no saying that at that moment the person wasn't watching them, and they both felt it was important not to hang around.

As they drove off, however, Emma smiled, thinking about the note Dan had left in the guestbook. Yes, they would return soon. She was determined about that.

They were half an hour into their drive – they had decided to head home and spend the last few days of their break relaxing in their flat – when Dan pulled off the main road. Emma knew from the signposts that they were now doubling back on themselves, heading south west instead of north east. He hadn't announced this change in route.

'Isn't this a different way from the one we came?' Emma ventured, knowing full well that it was. Dan was easy-going with most things in life, apart from driving. He didn't really like to be questioned about his driving ability even though, living in London, he rarely drove so was always slightly rusty behind the wheel. In fact, their worst ever falling-out had occurred during a fraught car journey, when Dan had got totally lost travelling through the Yorkshire Dales, yet had refused to accept the fact and ask for directions. Three hours later than planned, and by luck rather than design – or common sense – they had found the country hotel they had been heading for. They'd argued bitterly about that one.

'I've got a little surprise,' he replied. 'It's not too much of a diversion. I hope you don't mind.'

'Of course not.' Emma wondered what the surprise was. It struck her as slightly strange that Dan had chosen to do this, rather than just get home as soon as possible, but she didn't press him.

They travelled on for several more miles down country roads. Emma found herself closing her eyes against the brightness of the sun. She must have fallen asleep, because all of a sudden, when she next looked around, she was faced with a wall of densely packed trees on either side of the car, which was rocking and rolling along a dirt track of a road.

She looked across at Dan for an explanation of where they were, but he didn't seem to notice that she was awake – his eyes remained fixed on the road ahead. Maybe it was the disorientation of just waking, combined with the shock of their present, creepy environment, but a ridiculous thought entered her head.

Those who knew we were holidaying in Cornwall – Dan missed someone off the list.

Himself.

13

Emma pushed the ludicrous thought away.

And yet it's true.

Now Dan did notice that she was awake. Shadows from the forest they were driving through flashed across his face as he glanced across to her. 'I'm really sorry. I had no idea that the road would be like this. On the website, it said it was only a mile and a half from the main road. But I'm sure it's already been two.'

The car bumped hard as it hit a deep pothole.

Now Emma did ask the question, trying unsuccessfully to banish the sinister thoughts from her head. 'Where are we trying to get to?'

Dan went to answer, but he stopped as he noticed something in his rear-view mirror. 'Damn!'

Emma, already on edge, twisted round so quickly that she cricked her neck. There was a dark car behind them, fifty or so metres down the track. The glare from the sun, along with the shadows of the trees, meant that it wasn't possible to see the make of vehicle, never mind who was behind the wheel.

Dan shook his head. 'That's the last thing I need. Someone coming up behind us, putting on the pressure.'

'Maybe let him pass?'

Dan laughed. 'There hasn't been a passing point since the main road.'

'Oh.'

'Shouldn't be too much longer,' he said, just before they hit another pothole. They both nearly hit the car roof. He grimaced. 'Sorry.'

Emma looked at the car in the passenger side mirror. It wasn't getting any closer. But in some ways, that made it feel all the more menacing – even though she knew really that the likelihood was that there was nothing untoward.

If only I could see who was driving.

Emma pulled out her phone, about to use Google Maps to locate their position, but there was no phone signal, as was so common in Cornwall's more secluded spots. She was just about to enquire again as to their destination, when Dan broke into a smile.

'At last. We're here.'

The road suddenly opened out into a clearing. To their left was a low-rise building, which looked more modern than you might have expected in this isolated location. They passed a wooden sign.

Welcome to Dew Valley Vineyard.

Emma smiled. 'I've heard about this place.' She couldn't quite remember how she knew about it, but it was definitely familiar.

'You had a glass of one of their wines a few months ago,' Dan explained. 'When we went out for Lizzy's birthday.'

'Of course!' A very helpful waitress had recommended it. Both Emma and Lizzy had sung its praises, and they had looked for it, unsuccessfully, in the shops. 'I can't believe you remembered about that.'

'I made a note,' Dan said, swinging into the empty gravel car park that ran alongside the right-hand side of the building. 'We'd already talked about holidaying in Cornwall, so I thought it was worth remembering in case we had a chance to visit and buy some wine direct from source.'

Emma nodded, impressed.

'Their website was very helpful. Apart from the inaccurate distances.'

They crunched to a stop. Only when she heard the other car approach did Emma remember about the vehicle that had been following them. It parked over in the far corner, and a lean, tall guy in jeans and a T-shirt jumped out and jogged over to them.

'Hi,' he said, meeting them at the car door. He was in his late thirties, with stubble. 'Welcome to Dew Valley.' He held out his hand, which Dan shook. 'I'm Alex, Alex Dean. Sorry, I'm only just opening up. Kirsty was supposed to be manning the shop, but she's ill today. As soon as I found out, I came straight over, but I live ten miles away.'

'Don't worry,' Dan said. 'We'd only just arrived.'

'I've just got to do a couple of things inside.' Alex jogged off ahead to unlock the building.

'He's the co-owner,' Dan said, as they followed him. 'I remember the name from the website.'

'Really? He's so young.'

'Started the business in his early thirties, after a career in the City as a stockbroker.'

'Another person who dreamed of escaping the Big Smoke,' Emma noted.

As they neared the building, Emma felt guilty about her momentary lapse, where she had thought ill of Dan.

How can I have doubted him?

She took his hand and gave him a silent apology.

'We're now open for business,' Alex said, holding the door open for them as they entered. 'Feel free to ask any questions. Or ask for a sample. I'll just be over there.' He gestured towards the tasting bar and cash desk. 'And if you'd like to step out onto the veranda to admire the view, be my guest. I'm afraid we don't run tours on Sundays, but you can get a nice, wide-angle look at the vineyard.'

'Thanks,' Emma said, taking in the room. The open-plan space was filled with bottles of wine, either stacked up around the edges or in four displays at the centre of the room. They produced a lot of varieties, and Dan and Emma spent ten minutes or so browsing among them.

They moved out onto the veranda. 'Wow,' Dan said. The view was spectacular – spread out down below them in a bowl-shaped hollow of a valley were row after row of vines, basking in the autumn sunshine.

'I was so relieved,' Emma said, in a hushed tone, 'to find out that it was him following us.'

Dan got the insinuation. 'You thought it might be—?' The thought obviously hadn't occurred to him.

'Well, yes. Maybe.'

Dan blew out his cheeks as he rested against the wooden railings. 'That must have been scary.'

'It was. That, coupled with the fact that we were in the middle of nowhere, freaked me out for a couple of minutes.'

'Sorry,' he said. 'We should have gone straight back home.'

'No, it's okay, really,' she reassured him, touching his arm. 'I'm glad we came here. It was a lovely surprise.'

He appeared sufficiently convinced.

After a few minutes they moved back inside. 'I think that's the one,' Emma said, picking out the bottle. 'I seem to recognise the name.'

Dew Hill White Lady.

'You can taste to be sure,' Dan said at her shoulder. 'Then if that's the one, we can stock up.'

'Well, maybe just a little taste.'

It was the right wine. Or one that tasted so similar as to be indistinguishable from the one they had enjoyed in London. They bought four bottles – two for them and two for Lizzy – as well as a couple of bottles of a lovely rosé wine.

'So, you got what you came for?' Alex asked, boxing up the wine.

'Yes,' Emma said. 'Thanks.'

'Excellent.' He finished off with a strip of brown tape along the top of the box, and pushed it towards them. 'There you go.'

'Do you get much custom?' Dan asked. 'Being so far off the main road?' They were still the only customers in the building.

'In summer, yes. A lot. In July and August sometimes there's not enough space in the car park. Out of peak season, not so much in terms of people through the door. There are the regulars, of course – local people from Cornwall, and also Devon. They come all year round. But most walk-through custom is from holidaymakers, who've heard about us and take the opportunity to visit while they're staying in the area or passing through. That's why we have the vineyard tours – it brings people in. To be honest though, we couldn't survive solely on walk-through custom. Our biggest income generator is direct supply to restaurants. We're a major supplier to a lot of restaurants across the country, but particularly London. A few years back we did a lot of hard graft to develop relationships, and it paid off.'

'Sounds good,' Emma commented. 'That's how we discovered your wine – in a London restaurant. I really liked it, so Dan brought me here as a surprise.'

Alex smiled. 'Good. Nice to hear that. Otherwise I would have rushed over here to open up for nobody. Although,' he added, looking over towards the door, 'I was expecting at least one more customer. The guy on the motorbike. No idea where he went.'

'What do you mean?' Emma said.

'Didn't you see him? I passed him by the side of the road, just before I spotted you up ahead. I assumed he was just checking something, or taking a break. He didn't ask me to stop, so I don't think he had broken down. But now I'm not so sure.'

Emma didn't like the sound of this. 'Why do you think he might have broken down?'

'Well, because he hasn't arrived here. It's very strange.'

Dan interjected – he knew what Emma was thinking. 'Maybe he wasn't heading for here.'

Alex shook his head. 'The road doesn't lead to anywhere else. I guess maybe he was lost. He could have turned around once he realised. That's probably why he'd stopped.' He nodded at the plausibility of his own hypothesis.

But as much as Emma wanted to believe that explanation, she wasn't convinced. 'Did you see what he looked like?'

He was surprised by her level of interest. 'He had his crash helmet and the visor was down – I thought he must be rather hot like that – so, no, I couldn't see his face.'

'But you know it was a man?'

Alex blushed slightly. 'The leathers were tight. If it had been a woman, I would have known. Why do you ask?'

'She's just nosy,' Dan joked, before Emma could think how to respond.

'I know what you're thinking,' Dan said, starting the car engine as they belted up. 'But the likelihood is that it's nothing to worry about.'

'I know,' Emma replied. 'But it might be. Why else would that person be coming down that road, if it isn't to come to the vineyard?'

'As the guy said, maybe he got lost.'

'Maybe.'

Dan looked over towards the exit. 'I wish there was another way out, but there isn't.'

Emma shrank down into her seat. 'I know. Let's just get out of here. Being in the middle of the forest, cut off from the outside world with no phone signal ... it's giving me the creeps.'

Dan nodded. He pushed down on the central locking button. 'I'll drive as quickly as I can, and we're not going to stop for anyone. Okay?'

'Okay.'

They set off back through the trees down the dirt track. Dan was going faster than before, but he still had to keep the car below thirty, so as not to risk an accident – the track was just too uneven to push the car any more. And the last thing they wanted was to crash: as there was still no phone signal, in that event their only option would be to walk back either to the vineyard or to the main road. With the thought of the motorcyclist possibly lying in wait, both scenarios filled Emma with dread. She scanned the road ahead fearfully, as they bumped along, for signs of the man. But there was nothing.

They came to a sharp left-hand turn that Dan remembered from their inward journey. 'We're almost back on the main road,' he said, with notable relief.

Emma had thought that he had been relatively unconcerned by the situation, but she now could see she was wrong.

'Shit!' Dan suddenly slammed on the brakes as a 4x4 coming in the opposite direction barrelled towards them, going into a slight skid as it, too, braked sharply. They were both thrown forward, braced by their taut seatbelts.

The two vehicles came to a halt only a couple of metres apart. The driver of the 4x4, an older man, didn't look concerned by the near miss. He put up a hand and steered his vehicle around them, cutting across the wooded verge on the side of the track.

Emma breathed a huge sigh of relief. 'That was close.'

Dan, wide-eyed, rested on the steering wheel, recovering. 'Tell me about it.'

'If we'd hit this bend just a split second later, then, well, I hate to think what would have happened.'

'Don't . . . Put it this way, he was *a lot* bigger than us.' Dan raised himself back upright, realising the precarious position that they were in: 'We'd better not stay here, in case someone else comes flying round the corner.' He cranked the car into gear. 'Let's get out of here and get back onto that main road.'

'Good idea.'

He stepped out from behind the trees as Emma and Dan's car passed by, being careful to keep himself from view until they had gone around the corner. Smiling, he retrieved the motor-bike from its resting place beside a big oak and swung a leg over the powerful machine. Snapping his visor shut, he watched as a

4x4 rumbled by, before firing the ignition and cruising back down towards the main road. He would catch up with them in time. There wasn't any rush.

He knew where they were headed.

14

Emma and Dan arrived back just after five o'clock, weary and still dejected following the early ending of their holiday and the circumstances that had prompted it. The journey back had been without further incident, although Emma had scrutinised every motorbike that had passed them.

'There's nothing to say the guy on the motorbike was following us,' Dan had soothed. But despite his reassurance, she still had grave doubts.

They were surprised to find Lizzy waiting for them on their arrival. She had a spare key, which Emma had given her in case of emergencies, and had taken the liberty of starting an evening meal.

'I won't stay,' she said, somewhat apologetically, as she embraced Emma at the doorway. 'I don't want to cramp your style. But I thought you might appreciate the meal. It's lasagne with garlic bread.'

They hauled their bags into the flat, dumping them on the wooden boards of the hallway. 'Thanks, Lizzy,' Emma said. 'You really didn't need to do this, you know.'

'Yeah,' Dan added. 'It's a lot of effort.'

Lizzy shrugged it off. 'I didn't make it. It's a Waitrose special.'

In truth, they were both extremely grateful for her act of kindness. They'd had a service-station snack at the halfway point of their journey, but that was hours ago and they were famished. The thought of cooking something from scratch hadn't been appealing.

All three walked through into the kitchen. The smell coming from the oven was delicious.

Lizzy glanced at her watch. 'I'd better be going now. The meal will be ready in thirty minutes. Bon appétit!'

'Do you have to dash off?' Emma said.

'Er, I've not got anything planned. But don't you guys need some space?' She looked across at Dan questioningly.

'Stay,' Dan said. 'There'll be enough to go round.'

'I doubt it.' Lizzy snorted. 'It's not that big.'

'Then we'll chuck in a pizza,' Dan said. 'Mix and match.'

This time Lizzy looked at Emma. 'Are you sure?'

'Of course! It will be good to have the company.'

'Okay,' she said. 'Is it okay if we invite Will over? I know he's on his own tonight.'

'Sure,' Dan said, 'the more the merrier. Let's try to recreate the holiday atmosphere. And, anyway, it gives me an excuse not to unpack yet.' He smiled at Emma. 'And you know how much I hate unpacking.'

Will came straight over. While he was on his way, Emma told Lizzy all about what had happened over the weekend. She already knew the basic facts from when Emma had rung her to say they were on their way home, but was keen to hear things in greater detail. But she didn't say much, and Emma sensed that her best friend was holding something back.

Emma had the same feeling thirty minutes later, during the meal.

'So that's everything,' she said, as the four of them faced each other across the kitchen table, tucking into the lasagne and pizza. A bottle of the rosé from the vineyard was open in front of them, but no one had touched it as yet.

'I still can't believe that this person said his name was Stephen Myers.' Lizzy looked disturbed. 'I can't believe it.' She glanced across at Will.

'What is it?' Emma said, noting the look in Will's eyes.

There's definitely something going on.

'You'd better just tell them,' Will said.

'Tell us what?'

Lizzy grabbed the bottle of wine and poured herself a generous glass. 'I need some of this.' She took a gulp before replacing her glass on the table. 'Now, Em, this is going to sound crazy, and I can't believe I'm actually going to say it . . . but what if the person who you saw, the person who sent you those flowers, and who said he was Stephen Myers, what if it actually *is* Stephen Myers?'

Emma half laughed and exchanged a glance with Dan. 'We went through exactly the same thinking when we were in Cornwall. But it's just ridiculous to think that, isn't it?'

Lizzy didn't look like she was joking.

'What? You're not serious, are you?'

Lizzy held up her hands. 'I know, I know, it sounds mad. I told you it would be.'

Emma was stunned. She put down her knife and fork. 'I don't understand how you can really think that! Stephen Myers is dead. We saw his grave, remember? We stood there, next to Peter Myers, and looked at his headstone. He's been dead for over four years.'

'I know.' Lizzy seemed to be struggling with what she was trying to say. 'I know we saw that, but . . .'

Emma looked at Will again. He was solemn and avoided eye contact. 'Something's happened. Tell me what.'

Will exhaled and looked up at the ceiling.

'Will, please . . .'

He turned towards his sister. 'That journalist who's been following us around, Adrian Spencer. Yesterday he told Lizzy something.'

He paused, and Lizzy picked up the story. 'He followed me onto a bus, on my way to the theatre. At first he was just trying to convince me again to give me a quote for his feature story, but when we got off the bus, and I told him to get lost, he told me something.'

'Go on.'

'He said that as part of the research for the piece, he'd been to speak to Peter Myers in prison. And Peter Myers told him that Stephen isn't dead.'

Lizzy's claim was met with disbelief by Emma. '*What?* Isn't dead? But . . . of course he's dead.' Faced with that terrifying thought, she was floundering. She turned to Will. 'But you saw him. You saw his body.'

Will looked away.

Emma looked to Dan for support.

'But you did, didn't you?' Dan said. 'You saw him. You . . . you got rid of the body.'

'I *know* what I did!' Will half shouted. He looked at them in turn, his expression pained. 'I know what I did,' he repeated, muttering under his breath.

'Then I don't understand,' Emma said softly, recognising Will's distress. 'How can you think that he might be alive, just because Peter Myers said it?'

Will rubbed his hand down his cheek. 'Because I didn't see his face.' Suddenly he looked tearful. 'When I was there that night, in the flat, I couldn't bring myself to look at him properly. I'd never seen a dead body before, so I didn't look too closely. Stuart dealt with most of it until we had him, you know, wrapped up, in the sheets. So I don't know for certain that it was him.'

'But you've never had these doubts before,' Emma said.

'I know. But I've had no reason to doubt it. But now I do – after what happened with you and Dan in Cornwall, and after what Peter Myers said.'

Emma shook her head. 'The police would have made sure they had the right person.'

'They can make mistakes,' Lizzy said. 'I've heard stories of mistaken identity – you know, they bury the wrong person, or they think that the body they've found is someone who it isn't.'

'I didn't think it would be possible, either,' Will said. 'But as Lizzy said to me, by the time the police found the body, it had been in the water for days. It might not, you know, have been that easy to recognise. Maybe they just assumed it was him.'

Emma didn't really believe that. 'But they can check dental records, can't they? Or DNA? They don't just go by assumptions, surely.' She looked across at Dan.

He looked pensive. 'I suppose if the identification was made by a close relative, then maybe they leave it at that.'

Emma didn't like the idea at all. 'You mean Peter Myers might have deliberately misidentified the person as Stephen?'

'I've got no idea,' he admitted. 'But it's possible, maybe.'

Emma shook her head. 'I still think Peter Myers is just playing games with us again. He knows how to get at us, even when he's locked up in jail.'

Dan nodded. 'You're probably right.'

'Yes, I guess so,' Will admitted.

Emma focused on her best friend. 'Lizzy, you don't think so?'

Lizzy shrugged.

Emma had another idea. 'Adrian Spencer might be making it up, trying to get us to talk. Maybe he hasn't spoken to Peter Myers at all – he's just trying to provoke a reaction.'

Lizzy closed her eyes. 'No, that's not it.'

'But how can you be so sure?'

Lizzy sighed as she opened her eyes again. 'Because he told me the same thing.'

'Who?'

'Peter Myers. When he was holding me captive – he told me that Stephen was alive. He told me that the person who Stuart had killed wasn't his son.'

'What? Why didn't you *tell* us?' Emma said, shocked that her friend had kept that from her. But then why should she be surprised? Lizzy had been through the same traumatic experience as Dan, and, like him, she hadn't said much about anything that had happened inside Peter Myers' house.

Emma really knew nothing about what had gone on inside that house of horrors.

'Because I thought it was rubbish,' Lizzy responded. 'I thought it was just the ranting of a madman. And I also thought if you knew what he'd said, it would just freak you out. I was going to tell you, a few weeks ago, but then you became so anxious, thinking you were seeing Stephen Myers when we were out shopping, for instance. I thought that telling you that would make things worse. And I thought that's just what he would have wanted, to scare you – to bring the one you fear back from the dead.'

Emma pondered on Lizzy's reasoning. If the roles had been reversed, she realised she would have probably done the same thing. 'I'm sorry, Lizzy, for reacting the way I did. I understand why you didn't tell me.'

'I am sorry, Em.'

'It's okay, honestly.'

Now it was Will's turn to speak again. 'Tell her what else Peter Myers said.'

Emma turned to Lizzy once again, warily this time. 'What else did he tell you?'

Lizzy hesitated.

'Tell us,' Dan directed. 'We need to know everything.'

Lizzy took another drink of wine and steadied herself. 'I'm really sorry to have to tell you this, Em.' She looked at Emma. 'He said that Stephen Myers was coming back for you.'

'He can't be alive,' Emma said, as they sat nervously in the living room after dinner. The television was on, with some costume drama showing, but none of them was really taking it in. 'He *can't* be.'

The others remained silent, letting her statement hang in the air.

'Think back,' she said to Will, 'to the night Stuart called you over. You might not have looked at Stephen's face, but Stuart told you it was him, didn't he?'

Will looked like the last thing he wanted to do was to think back to those horrific events, and Emma didn't like making him revisit his painful past, but it was important. 'Yes, he told me that it was Stephen Myers. No doubt about it.'

'Well, why would he say it was Stephen Myers if it was really someone else?'

'I don't know. He wouldn't, I guess.'

'Exactly. There was no reason for him to lie.'

'But the person in Cornwall—' Lizzy said.

'Was someone impersonating Stephen Myers,' said Emma, firmly. 'I don't know who it is, or why, but it just can't really be him.'

'Em's right,' Will said. 'Stephen Myers is dead. He has to be.'

'But you said before . . .' Lizzy began.

'I got carried away,' Will said. 'If you think about it, it doesn't make sense.'

'Maybe,' Lizzy replied, 'but it still leaves someone else out there, pretending to be him.'

'That's what worries me,' said Dan. 'I'm not really concerned about Stephen Myers – he's long gone. I'm worried about the person who is living and breathing – the person who was following us in Cornwall. I'm worried that he might now be in London. And I'm worried about what his motivations are, and what he might do next.'

Emma closed her eyes at the thought and shook her head gently.

'It's okay, Em,' Lizzy said, taking her hand. 'We're all in this together. We've all got to be strong, and face it, just like we were strong the first time.'

'Lizzy's right,' Dan said. 'We've got to stick together.'

'I'm in, no question about it,' Will said. 'Someone's trying to scare you, Em, and it's not right. We're not going to let them do this.'

'So what do we do?' Lizzy said. 'Call the police?'

Emma nodded. 'I think we should. We didn't call them in Cornwall, because we thought it was best to wait until we got back here, and spoke to officers who know the background.'

'Emma's right,' Dan said. 'Now we're back, I don't see any reason for delaying telling them.'

'I think we should call Gasnier directly,' Lizzy said. 'Don't you?'

Knowing how Lizzy felt about Detective Inspector Mark Gasnier, Emma was surprised at her suggestion. Lizzy had taken an uncharacteristic dislike to him: 'arrogant' had been one of her more flattering descriptions of the police officer who had led the hunt for Dan.

Lizzy held up her hands, noting Emma's surprise. 'Okay, I know what I said about him, and I still don't like the guy. But he knows us, and he knows the case. He might be more likely to give us a hearing.'

'She's got a point,' Will said. 'He might help.'

Emma looked questioningly at Dan.

'Call him,' said Dan. 'If someone's following you again, we can't just sit back and wait to see what happens. And if Gasnier can do something about it, then let's try and get him involved.'

Five minutes later they had their answer.

'Not that interested,' Emma said, deflated, as she ended the call.

Lizzy shook her head. 'I should have known. Sorry, Em.'

'Not interested at all?' Will said.

Emma placed the phone on the arm of the sofa. 'He said just to be aware of things, not take any unnecessary risks, report anything more sinister if it happens, and then they can take action.'

Dan snorted. 'Basically, it was a total waste of time, then. Sometimes I wonder whether the police actually want to prevent crimes.'

'Now what?' Lizzy said.

Emma shrugged. 'Keep our eyes open, I guess, and be careful.'

'Hire a private detective,' Will put in. 'They could follow you, to see if you are being stalked by this person.'

Lizzy looked interested. 'Hey, that's not a bad idea.'

'I don't like the thought of a private investigator,' Emma replied. 'It sounds too heavy. And, anyway, aren't they expensive, even if we did know a good one to approach?'

'Probably,' Dan said. 'To be honest, you don't really need a private eye. You just need someone who can follow you, keep their eye out, and maybe take a few photographs of anyone who looks suspicious.'

'Follow and take photographs . . .' Lizzy clicked her fingers. 'I've got an idea.'

15

Adrian Spencer woke early. He popped out before breakfast to get a *Telegraph*, before returning to his flat and scanning the day's news. He was halfway through the paper when his mobile rang. It was only 8 a.m. – very early for someone to be calling about business, surely. He considered not answering, but changed his mind after consulting the screen and seeing the caller ID.

This should be fun.

He spoke through a mouthful of toast. 'Adrian Spencer.'

He listened, without a reply, for the next minute and a half as the caller ranted at him.

My God, they're really losing it.

When they'd stopped he remained silent, a smile flickering across his lips as he thought about the reaction on the other end of the line.

The ranting started again.

'I'm sorry,' he said, cutting in curtly, 'but, really, as I've explained to you already, it's too late. There's no going back now. You've sold your story, and now it's too late.'

Now the caller was pleading. He moved the phone away from his ear, but it was still possible to hear the sob story. It was so tiresome. Adrian looked over at the rest of his breakfast. He was also in the middle of a very interesting article, which he was keen to get back to. 'Listen,' he said, eventually. 'You're wasting your time. Please, just move on.'

He ended the call before they had a chance to reply.

He resumed eating, and finished the article. It was a story about a young British guy who was unicycling across the United

States for charity. Having started on the West Coast early the previous year, he was now only a day away from his final destination, New York City. The American public had taken him in as one of their own and he'd been lauded on several of the big American television networks. Yet this was the first Adrian had heard of him. As far as he knew, there had been no mention of him in the UK press.

Oh, how we neglect our good news.

Not that he could criticise. He'd spent his whole career making a living off the misfortune of others.

He finished his breakfast and retrieved his hand-held digital recorder from the bottom of his work bag. Finding the correct file, he was just about to press play when his phone rang again.

'Not again.'

But it wasn't them.

'Hi, Adrian Spencer here . . . Yes, I've been up for a while. How are you? . . . Good to hear it . . . I think the research is going remarkably well, after what I'll admit was quite a slow start . . . Of course, yes, but if you consider where we were at just a few days ago, then it's a big step forward to have one of Emma Holden's inner circle on board . . . Okay, sure. I'll call you later and let you know.'

Adrian had managed to hide his anger.

Really, is there any need to check up on me each and every morning? Is that what this has come to?

He was being treated like a junior, not the experienced professional that he was.

He paced around the flat, mulling things over in his head.

Okay, it hasn't gone well to start with, although that certainly isn't through a lack of effort on my part. And now, as I said, it's really turned a corner.

'So annoying.'

He sat back down and began playing the digital audio file of the conversation he had had with the person who knew Emma so well. It cheered him up immensely.

It was gold.

He folded his arms behind his head, leant back in his chair, and enjoyed each and every word. It was so much better than even he could have hoped. It had been a flawless performance on his part – one of his best ever. No wonder they were now backtracking.

'If only you knew the truth,' he said, smiling, as the recording continued. 'You think you feel bad now . . .'

'Oh . . . it's you.'

Standing at his front door on that bright Monday morning, David Sherborn was visibly shocked. More than that, he looked horrified, which, given their recent history, was completely understandable. The photographer who had been paid by Guy Roberts to follow Emma, getting photographs for Guy's perverse publicity campaign for his movie, probably hadn't expected to ever see them back at his house.

'Hi,' Emma said, trying for a well-intentioned smile. 'Sorry to just turn up unannounced. Could we come in and have a quick chat?'

He glanced around, biting his lip. 'The family are in. Let's go around to my studio, where we spoke last time.'

As he had done just over a month ago, he led them around the side of the house to the rear studio annexe. The visit certainly brought back all the memories for Emma, and no doubt it did the same for David Sherborn.

Lizzy's idea – to try and enlist his help – had been an inspired one, and had met with instant agreement from the other three. Sherborn had already demonstrated his ability to follow people around and take photos; whether he would agree to do such a thing for them was another matter.

The decision for only Lizzy and Emma to visit him, rather than bring along Dan, was a calculated one; introducing some-one new, particularly male, might scare him off. Instead, Dan had decided to go into the office and save that day's holiday for another time. But they were under strict instructions to call him at any time, should anything happen.

'Take a seat,' Sherborn said, still looking nervous. 'Can I get you a drink? Tea, coffee? I've got a new espresso machine – I can do cappuccinos, lattes . . .'

'Lattes,' said Emma, knowing Lizzy's favourite drink. 'Thanks.'

'I'll just be a second.'

Emma and Lizzy waited on the studio's sofa as David Sherborn disappeared through the door to the left. They both looked around. Over in the far corner, leaning up against the wall, was a set of large prints of a smiling young family. Emma thought that the little girl in the shots was incredibly cute. The photos were stunning – the energy coming from them was so tangible. Then, in the opposite corner, Emma noticed a print of Tower Bridge. It was taken at night and was very atmospheric. There was no doubt that David Sherborn was an extremely talented photographer.

It made his decision to have acted as a paparazzo and scare them to death all the sadder.

'Did you see his face?' Lizzy whispered, leaning in close to Emma as she continued to admire David Sherborn's work. 'He didn't look pleased to see us, did he?'

'No, he didn't,' Emma replied, glancing over towards the door, worried that he might come back through and overhear their conversation – this situation was uncomfortable enough without something like that happening. She dropped her voice even more. 'I hope we're doing the right thing.'

'He can only say no,' Lizzy said.

'I know.'

Lizzy smiled. 'But I don't think he will.'

Lizzy had been confident that David Sherborn would agree to their request, but Emma wasn't so sure.

'So,' said Sherborn, returning and handing them their cups. 'What can I do for you?'

Emma felt sorry for him. He seemed to have calmed down a little, but he still didn't look quite at ease. Who knew what was going through his mind at that moment?

'We need your help,' Emma said.

That obviously took him by complete surprise. 'Oh. I thought it might be about what happened, you know, with, well, you know what I mean.' He looked down towards his feet, blushing.

'It is, in a way,' Emma said.

'Oh?'

She cleared her throat. 'We think that someone else might be following me, stalking me. And they're pretending to be Stephen Myers.'

He sat forward. 'An impersonator?'

'Yes.'

'Oh, right, that's . . . awful. I'm really sorry to hear that.'

'Something happened while Dan and I were on holiday in Cornwall at the weekend. Someone sent me some flowers, pretending to be Stephen Myers. And I think they also followed me and Dan when we were on a night out. I think I've seen the person in London too, about two weeks ago. I thought it was just my imagination, but now I think that there really was somebody there.'

'I can see how that would be disconcerting. You've told the police?'

'They can't really do anything,' Lizzy said. 'No crime has been committed. They've just advised us to be alert, and report anything else that happens. Then they might be able to act. I think it's the usual stuff that they do in the early stages of things like this.'

'But with everything that's happened, if there's someone out there, won't they act?'

Emma shrugged. 'I don't think they're too concerned at the moment.'

'And in the meantime,' Lizzy added, 'we're left wondering who this person is, and why he's doing it.'

'Right . . .' Suddenly Sherborn's face flushed with horror. 'You don't think this has got anything to do with me, do you? I mean, I know what I did, and I'm so sorry for it, I really am. But I promise this has nothing to do with me. Nothing. I swear.'

'It's okay,' Emma said hurriedly. 'We don't think you've got anything to do with it. That's not why we're here.'

'That's a relief,' he said, running a hand across his forehead and into his hair. 'You know, it's been a difficult few weeks, trying to come to terms with what I did. I still feel really ashamed. I never told my wife, although I've thought maybe I should. I gave the money away, you know. The money I was paid, to follow you and take the photos – I've given it to charity. Great Ormond Street Hospital are running an appeal.'

'That's great,' Emma said.

He shrugged. 'Well, it was the least I could do.' He looked away again, his hands clasped in front of him as if he was in a confessional.

'You really helped us,' Emma said. 'Without you telling us about Guy Roberts and what he was doing, we might not have found Dan.'

'Sorry, I didn't even ask how your boyfriend is. I saw the reports in the newspapers that he'd been found.'

'He's okay now. But the events of the past few days have set us all back a little.'

'I can imagine.' David seemed to remember something. 'You said you needed my help?'

Emma smiled. 'Yes, we do.'

He looked quizzical. 'I don't understand. What can I do?'

'I want to know if there is definitely someone following me – we all want to know,' Emma said. 'And if there is someone, then I want to know who. The police won't help yet, but we hope that you might.'

'I don't understand what you mean.'

'We want to ask you a favour. We want you to follow me, take photographs and see if there is anyone stalking me.'

David Sherborn laughed incredulously. 'I'm not a private detective . . .'

'It's only what you did four weeks ago,' Lizzy said. 'Following Emma, taking photographs, staying out of sight. Except that this time, you'd be doing it for the right reasons.'

'Aren't you forgetting,' he said, after a few seconds of contemplation, 'that I wasn't very good at it. You found me out, remember?'

'Only after a while,' Emma replied. 'By then, you'd already been following me for days, hadn't you? And you'd already got lots of photographs.'

He nodded. 'That's true, yes.'

'Whereas this time you would only need to do it for a few days, maybe just two or three – long enough to be sure whether someone is following me. And if you get photographs, we could give them to the police and maybe they could then take action.'

'Taking police matters into your own hands ... it sounds dangerous.'

'It wouldn't be,' Lizzy said. 'If there is someone following Emma, we don't want you to engage with them in any way. And we don't want you to follow *them* – only Emma. We don't want anyone put in danger, and that includes you.'

It looked to Emma and Lizzy as if there was an internal battle waging as Sherborn considered his response. 'Work's getting busy again,' he said, eventually. 'I've been trying to put all this behind me, and I've got a queue of clients for family portraits.' He gestured over to the canvas prints that they had been admiring. 'The second half of this week I'm pretty full with bookings.'

Clearly, he was leading up to a 'no'. But Lizzy, the most determined person that Emma had ever met, wasn't giving in just yet. 'What about the first half of the week?'

'Quieter,' he replied, after a slight hesitation. 'I've got some night-time shoots, but during the day today through till Wednesday, it's clear at the moment.'

'That's all we'd need,' Lizzy said. 'Those three days. See if you can see anybody, hang back as far as you can with one of your telephoto lenses, shoot some pictures, then we can meet up later on Wednesday afternoon and see what you've got.'

'Please,' urged Emma. 'I'd be really grateful.'

He thought again. 'Okay,' he said finally. 'I'll do it. And I won't take any money for it.' He seemed to relax now the decision had been made.

'Thank you so much!' Emma smiled with relief.

'Yes, that's great!' Lizzy echoed.

That brought out his first real smile of the meeting. 'So, how is this going to work? You want me to follow you around the whole time?'

'As much as you can,' Emma said.

'What if I lose you?'

'We'll text you regularly,' Emma said. 'Let you know where I am. And you can always call me if there's a problem.'

He nodded. Now he looked really happy. 'I *am* glad to be able to help, you know. I still feel like I owe you.'

16

'That went well,' Lizzy said, as they walked back towards the tube station.

'Seemed to, yes,' Emma agreed. 'You don't think he felt forced into it?'

'Nah . . . well, maybe a little.' Lizzy smiled naughtily. 'But, hey, did you see the way he looked by the time we left? He was happy.'

'You're right,' Emma agreed. 'He did look really happy.'

'Well, there you go, then,' Lizzy said, patting Emma on the arm playfully. 'We kill two birds with one stone. David Sherborn is given an opportunity to redeem himself, and we get a private eye for free.'

'Except he's not a private eye, though, is he?'

'No, but you know what I mean. If someone is following you, then I think he'll spot them.'

'Me, too.'

They walked on, as the man watched from a safe distance.

They travelled from David Sherborn's house into the centre of town, hitting the shops on Oxford Street.

They went first to Hamleys toy store. Lizzy wanted to pick up a present for her three-year-old nephew. She decided on a battery-operated wooden train, knowing that he was mad about trains and had an extensive track at home. Having paid and left the store, they then headed for one of their favourite destinations.

'Ahh, retail therapy,' Lizzy said, as they entered John Lewis's flagship store, just down from Oxford Circus. 'You deserve it, after the weekend you've just had.'

Emma smiled back. 'I do, don't I?'

They worked the store from top to bottom, chatting and gossiping while they went. Emma for the most part managed to forget about her troubles. Their baskets remained empty, and they just enjoyed the browsing experience. That was until they reached the footwear department – Emma and Lizzy both had a weak spot when it came to shoes and boots.

'You're not going to buy those now, are you?' Lizzy asked, as Emma admired a pair of blue Hunter wellington boots.

'Maybe . . .'

'We're not far from Christmas,' Lizzy said. 'Put it on your list to Santa.'

'You're right. Dan always struggles to know what to buy me.' She placed the boots back on the display shelf. 'Just don't let me forget.'

'I won't.'

They had a coffee in the espresso bar, then picked up a few small items in the stationery department – another of Emma's weaknesses – before heading out.

'Lunchtime,' Lizzy announced, glancing at her watch as they exited. 'You hungry?'

'Enough for a sandwich.'

'Great. Shall we head up to Soho?'

'Soho? We could grab something in Marks, couldn't we?' Marks & Spencer was only just round the corner.

'There's a new vegetarian deli café that one of the girls was raving about the other day,' Lizzy explained. 'I think it's owned by a celebrity chef. Can't think of his name. According to Michelle, it's not expensive, but the food's amazing.'

'Sounds good.'

'Thanks for this,' Emma said as they sat in the deli café, snacking on their warm, sun-dried tomato, mozzarella and pesto paninis. 'I've really enjoyed this morning. And this place is really great.'

The small deli was delightful. It had a pastel green and white décor, with cool, light-box bright lighting. Lizzy's colleague had been right: the food was reasonably priced and tasted great.

'No worries whatsoever,' Lizzy said, swallowing a mouthful of food. 'I'm just happy to help. I thought the idea of the holiday in Cornwall was so good – it was just what you both needed. So I was gutted when you called with the news about what was happening. And then when you said you were coming home early, well, it was terrible.'

'I was really enjoying it,' Emma said. 'The apartment was amazing, and the view from our balcony was stunning. You could see right out to sea. St Ives was lovely, too. We're going to go back as soon as we can.'

'You should,' Lizzy replied. She shook her head. 'It makes me so angry that some idiot has spoilt things for you two. And what for? For a cheap thrill? I don't understand why someone would want to do that.'

'Me, neither.'

'Do you think he's here now?' Lizzy said.

Emma resisted the temptation to look around. 'Who? David Sherborn or the Stephen Myers impostor?'

'I was thinking more of the Stephen Myers impostor.'

Now Emma did look up. 'I hope not.' Scanning around as discreetly as she could, she looked at the other customers: a young mother sitting in the far corner, spooning food into her baby's open mouth; a couple of businessmen eating alone; two young friends who looked like they might be students; and a middle-aged woman who was reading a novel.

'You seem to be handling this really well,' Lizzy said. 'I mean, after all that you've already gone through, now to have this to deal with – it would be totally understandable if you felt it was all too much.'

Emma took another bite from her panini. 'I'm actually surprised myself. I can't explain why I feel calmer about it all, but I just do. Maybe it's because I know that the real danger, the person who nearly killed Richard and took Dan and you, is safely locked away.'

'But somebody *is* out there, pretending to be Stephen Myers. That must worry you.'

'It does. But I know I've got all of you with me. Dan's here now, you're here, and Will. Knowing you're all there gives me strength and makes me feel safe. Plus, whoever this person is, they want me to be scared, and I guess I don't want to give them what they're after.'

'You're stronger than people think,' Lizzy said. 'Quietly strong.'

Emma smiled. 'Thanks.'

Lizzy suddenly looked perturbed.

'What is it, Lizzy?'

She smiled sadly. 'I'm just really sorry, Em. For not telling you about what Peter Myers said to me about Stephen. I was just so torn. I didn't know what to do for the best.'

'It's okay, honestly. I know you did it for the right reasons. We can't let Peter Myers get to us. He can only hurt us if we let him.'

'It seems like he's using Adrian Spencer to do that – using him as a mouthpiece. I can't believe that he went to speak to him in prison. I mean, who would stoop so low as to speak to *that* man, and give him a platform? I mean, if you want to write a piece on what happened, then fine, but why seek out his views? The man is a monster. Why did the prison even let him speak to him?' She shook her head again, her eyes blazing. 'He's lower than the low, and he *shouldn't* have a voice. What he did to you, Dan, Richard and me . . . to us all . . .'

This was the first time Emma had seen Lizzy get emotional about the whole experience with Peter Myers. Maybe all those emotions and feelings that she had no doubt been bottling up were now surfacing.

Emma reached out her hand. 'I wish Adrian Spencer would just disappear. To be honest, I don't care any more if he writes his story or not. I just want him to leave us alone. Once the story is published, then that will be that, and we'll never hear from him again. And he can get all the quotes he likes from Peter Myers. But at least we know that none of us have talked.'

'Agreed,' Lizzy said. But she was uncharacteristically quiet as she finished off the rest of her lunch.

'You don't have to be strong all the time, you know,' Emma said. 'Not for my benefit, anyway.'

Lizzy knew what she meant. 'I know.' She sipped her glass of traditional lemonade. Emma knew that she was working her way up to saying something significant. 'When he grabbed me off the street, I thought that was going to be it.' She swallowed away tears as her lip trembled. 'I thought I was going to . . .'

'It's okay,' Emma said, squeezing her hand across the table. 'We don't have to discuss this now, if you don't want to.'

Lizzy screwed her eyes shut.

'I'm here for you, Lizzy. Just like you're always there for me.'

Lizzy nodded. 'I know that.'

'Let's talk about something else,' Emma suggested. There was no way she wanted to make Lizzy feel like this in public.

'It's okay,' Lizzy said, opening her eyes. No tears were falling. 'I do want to talk about it. I *need* to talk about it. I know I come across as all calm and controlled, but it's a bit of a brave face.' She went to say more, but stopped, shocked as she spotted the time on Emma's watch. 'Oh, hell, I'm late for the cast and crew meeting. They want to review how the show has gone so far, see if there's any room for improvement. It's a three-line whip. If I'm not there, there'll be trouble. Sorry, Em, I'm going to have to go.'

'It's okay, you go. Don't give that director any more ammunition. But we can talk more later, if you like.'

'Yes, I'd like that. You'll go straight home, won't you?' Lizzy grabbed her jacket and got to her feet. 'I don't like the idea of you walking around on your own, not at the moment.'

'I'll go straight back,' Emma replied. 'Don't worry. I'll finish my drink first, though.'

*　　*　　*

118

Emma watched as Lizzy exited the deli and hurried off past the window and down the street. She glanced around again at the other customers. They were all busy with their own business – talking between themselves or on their mobile phones, browsing the internet, or simply enjoying the food and drink. No one seemed interested in her. But still, now that Lizzy had gone, she felt exposed.

She'd just drained her glass when her phone rang. It wasn't a number she recognised.

'Hello?'

'Is that Emma? Emma Holden?'

'Yes, it's Emma.' The woman's voice on the other end of the line was instantly recognisable, even though it had been years. 'Charlotte, is that you?'

The caller seemed taken aback at the instant recognition. 'Yes, yes, it is.' Emma couldn't believe it: Charlotte Harris, Stuart's sister. 'I wondered if it would be possible to meet up.'

Emma was surprised. They hadn't been in contact since her break-up with Stuart. 'Okay, sure.'

'This afternoon if you can.'

'This afternoon?'

What is this about?

'I should have called you before now. It's really very important.'

17

Edward Holden stood in the middle of the bridge, gazing down at the shimmering water below, lost in thought. A few weeks before, on this very spot, he had revealed to Emma that Miranda was pregnant with his child. Despite his fears that it would result in the breakdown of his relationship with his daughter, she had taken it well – much better than he had imagined.

I should give my children more credit.

He bit down hard on his bottom lip as he tapped a finger against the railings. Behind him, London traffic sped past, oblivious to the pain that he was going through. He exhaled and looked up at the sky.

'What should I do?'

He reached down inside his jacket pocket and pulled out a white envelope, which was stuffed with banknotes. He didn't want to touch them.

Blood money.

He mused again on the amount of cash. It still seemed far too much. In fact, it made him deeply suspicious about the whole situation.

Is there more to this?

He held the envelope out over the drop and fantasised about letting it go and watching the money float down the river and out of his life.

But, of course, I could never do that.

Dissatisfied with his inability to carry out his imaginings, he shoved the envelope back into his jacket and set off back towards the house.

En route, he passed the Cancer Research UK charity shop. And that's when he knew what to do.

Following his wife's death from breast cancer, Emma and Dan had run the London Marathon on behalf of the charity. The shop had also received donations of her clothes.

He walked in, straight up to the counter. The shop was empty of customers, but there were two ladies behind the desk working their way through a box of bric-a-brac, which presumably had been dropped off by a member of the public.

Before Edward could change his mind, he brought out the envelope. 'I'd like to make a donation.'

The ladies smiled, but didn't look surprised. People came in with cash donations all the time. It was only when they noticed the thick pile of notes peeking out from inside the envelope that their expressions changed.

Except that they looked nervous, rather than pleased.

'It's okay,' Edward said. 'I've just come into some money. And I'd like to make a donation.' He held out the envelope, but they didn't take it. It was going to take more persuasion. And no wonder. A pile of banknotes probably wasn't the usual way of gifting. They probably suspected it wasn't legitimate, or it was just a joke. 'My wife, she died of cancer, you see.'

Edward, his hand still out, pleaded with his eyes for them to relieve him of his heavy load.

The women glanced at one another and one nodded. 'That's very generous,' the older of the two ladies said, turning back to him. 'But are you sure? It looks like a great deal of money.'

'It is,' Edward confirmed. 'And, yes, I'm sure. I've never been more certain about anything in my entire life.'

'Well, thank you so much,' the woman said, taking the money. She laid it down on a shelf behind them, in between a china doll and a rather worn teddy bear.

'Yes, thank you for your amazing generosity,' her colleague added.

He smiled. 'Don't mention it.' He turned to go.

'Excuse me!' the first lady called after him. 'Would you like a receipt?'

He paused at the door. 'It's fine.'

'I thought you might need it for tax purposes . . .'

Edward almost laughed at the irony. This was certainly something that he wasn't ever going to declare.

Edward reached home a few minutes later. He felt somewhat better, but not much. That's when he had another thought.

I've done some good, but it isn't enough.

He moved up to the bedroom, retrieved two travel bags from the wardrobe and proceeded to stuff them full of clothes and toiletries. Miranda was out at work, and would only be back after six, so he had the place to himself. There was no one to disturb him.

Just ten minutes later he stood at the front door, a bag in each hand.

'I'm sorry.'

He was crying by the time he reached the car. He sped off down the road without looking back.

Taking heed of Lizzy's warning not to go off anywhere on her own, Emma offered to meet Charlotte in the deli café. She ordered a pot of tea and a slice of carrot cake, hungry with nervous energy at the though tof the meeting. By the time she finished her second cup, Charlotte had arrived.

'Emma,' she said, unsmiling, standing over her at the table, a Gucci handbag hanging from one shoulder. 'It's been a long time.'

Emma stood up and the two kissed a polite hello. Charlotte had a cropped brown bob, which framed her pretty face. It replaced the long hairstyle that Emma remembered, and it suited her.

They both sat down, and Emma searched for some appropriate words. It felt awkward, being face to face again with Stuart's little sister. It had been years since she had last seen her – the day before Stuart had walked out on her, in fact. A group of them had picnicked in Hyde Park, and everything had seemed perfect – better than they'd been between her and Stuart for a while. There had been no warning signs, although now Emma knew that Stuart had been carrying the shockingly dark secret of Stephen Myers' murder around with him for some time before then: the secret that was to mean the end of them as a couple.

'Can I get you something to drink?' Emma managed.

'I'll have an orange juice.'

Emma ordered her drink from the waitress. 'You've really grown up,' she said to Charlotte.

Charlotte blushed slightly. 'Yes, I'm not a naïve little girl any more, that's for sure.'

'Sorry, I didn't mean that to sound patronising.'

'It's okay, it didn't.' Her juice arrived and she took a few sips.

Emma took a proper look at her. She had aged quite considerably in the intervening years. In fact, she looked significantly older than mid-twenties. Her skin looked as if she might be a smoker, and her eyes were tired.

How much of that aging has taken place in the weeks since Stuart's suicide?

'It's good to see you again,' Emma said.

'And you. Although I thought we might have seen you at Stuart's funeral.'

Emma was afraid she would mention that. 'I felt it would be better if I stayed away.' It had been a big surprise to receive an invitation, but she really hadn't felt able to go. It hadn't seemed right. She'd decided it would be better for everyone – not only herself, but also Dan, and Stuart's family for that matter – if she stayed away. So instead she'd sent a condolence card and given her apologies.

'Well, I would have liked to have seen you,' Charlotte replied.

'I . . .' Emma hesitated.

'I really missed you, you know, after you split with Stuart.'

'I missed you, too.' As was understandable, the end of her and Stuart's relationship had also meant the end of Emma's friendship with Charlotte. They'd actually been quite close. On a number of occasions, Charlotte had travelled down from the north west and stayed at their London flat, and Emma and Stuart had shown her the sights. She was a nice girl, five years younger than Emma, and she had felt like the little sister Emma had never had. Over the years, Emma had wondered what had become of her. And now here she was.

Charlotte seemed surprised. 'Did you really miss me?'

'Of course I did.'

She seemed to have trouble accepting that. 'You could have got in touch, you know. I mean, I know that Stuart broke up with you, but it didn't mean you had to just . . . abandon me.'

'I'm really sorry, Charlotte. I never knew you felt like that.'

'No, how could you?'

'I wish it had been that easy to stay in touch,' Emma said, 'but it wasn't. Stuart broke off all links with me, and I certainly don't think he would have wanted me to have any contact with you.'

'I used to think that you were just letting things settle down, and then you'd come and see me. I wanted to tell you how sorry I was about what had happened. When I heard you two had split up, it was the worst thing in the world. And when you just disappeared, well, it felt like you were dead.'

'I don't know what to say,' Emma replied. 'If I had known how much it hurt you, then I would have got in touch. Sent a card.'

Charlotte shrugged, looking around distractedly. 'Well, anyway, it doesn't matter now. That was a long time ago.'

Emma could see the hurt in the other girl's eyes, but she was still none the wiser about why she had wanted to see her after all this time. Maybe it was Stuart's death that had been the catalyst for her to seek out connections. Emma had done the same after her mother's death – visiting long-lost family friends and relatives, wallowing in memories of the one that was gone. 'I'm so sorry about what happened to Stuart. I loved your brother, and I never wanted to see him hurt. When I found out what had happened, it was awful.'

Charlotte smiled disbelievingly. 'Really?'

Emma was taken aback by her reaction.

Does she really think so little of me?

'Yes, really.'

'Then why did you lead him on?'

'Pardon?'

This is crazy.

'Why did you lead him on the way you did? Make him feel like he had a chance with you again?'

Is this why she wanted to meet, to voice her anger at what happened to Stuart, and to assign blame?

Emma didn't want this to turn into an argument, but she needed to set the record straight. 'I didn't lead him on.'

'You did! He spoke to me, after the date you had on the river boat down the Thames. He was so happy, he truly believed there was a chance you two could get back together.'

Emma shook her head – Charlotte had this all wrong, possibly blinded by family loyalty, or maybe misled by Stuart himself. 'That wasn't a date, Charlotte. It was an event promoting a film. I didn't even know Stuart was going to be there.'

Charlotte sidestepped this explanation. 'Are you saying you didn't have a good time with my brother that night? I saw the photos in the newspaper, and I know what he told me.'

Yet again, those photos were causing trouble, leading people to the wrong conclusions.

'I'm not saying I didn't have a good time. I'm not saying that at all. What I'm saying is that it wasn't planned, and it certainly wasn't a date. And I also didn't do anything to lead your brother on.'

'That's not how he saw it,' Charlotte scoffed.

Emma tried again. This was threatening to turn nasty – it really wasn't what she needed right now. 'Charlotte, I know how awful these past few weeks must have been for you. What happened was such a terrible shock – for me, too.'

'Now you *are* patronising me,' Charlotte shot back. But it proved to be her final offensive manoeuvre for, after a few moments of silence, her face softened with sadness. She played with the top of her glass, tracing her finger around the damp rim with a red-painted fingernail. 'You don't know what it's like to lose your big brother, the only person who you could totally depend on. I know he made a big mistake – more than one, in fact – but he was a good person, Emma. He was a *good*, kind person.'

'I know he was.' Emma reached across the table and tried to take her hand, but Charlotte recoiled, looking up tearfully as she did so.

'He told me once how much he regretted losing you. He said he'd do anything to turn back the clock and be with you again. That's why he was so happy, when he thought there might be a chance.'

'I'm sorry, Charlotte, but there was never a chance. I love Dan.'

'I know. I just wish he hadn't met you again. He'd moved on with things. He was happy with his girlfriend, and things were going well.'

'I wish he could have moved on, too. I honestly do.'

'I've got to go,' Charlotte said. 'But the reason why I wanted to see you was to give you this.' She reached into her bag and handed over a brown envelope, with Emma's name scrawled on the front. It looked like Stuart's handwriting.

'Two days after Stuart died, I received a parcel from him,' Charlotte explained. 'He'd written letters to me, my mum and dad, his girlfriend Sally and you.'

The package felt like a visitation of Stuart's ghost. She looked up at Charlotte, as if for guidance.

'You don't have to open it now,' said Charlotte. 'Do it in your own time. I'm sorry, I should have given this to you before now, but I was angry.' She stood up. 'I'll be going now. Would you like me to pay for my drink?'

'It's okay, I'll get it.'

Emma watched as she left the café. The letter felt like a ton weight in her hands.

Should I open it?

She decided not to, for now. It wasn't the sort of thing she wanted to look at in public. She wasn't sure she wanted to look at it at all, but the right place was certainly not there. So she slipped it into her bag and went to the counter to pay.

'That's fine,' the girl said, as Emma presented her debit card. 'You don't have anything more to pay.'

'What do you mean?'

'Your friend covered the tab. Paid cash for the lot.'

Emma thought she must have misheard. 'Friend?'

'Yes, the man who left a few minutes ago. He paid for everything.'

'He must have made a mistake. He wasn't with us.'

'I know,' the girl said. 'He was sitting over at the back on his own, but he definitely meant to pay for your order. He pointed you out specifically.'

'I don't understand, why would somebody do that?' And yet, even as Emma said this, she knew what had happened.

'I wouldn't argue with a free lunch.' The girl smiled at Emma. 'Looks like you've got yourself a fan.'

18

Miranda returned from the hospital just after six o'clock. It had been a tiring day at work. The pregnancy was really taking its toll, sapping her energy levels to the extent that, for most of the day, she had just wanted to curl up in a corner and sleep. But her schedule afforded no time for rest: as a doctor, she knew the needs of the patients came before her own. Now, however, she wanted to relax – maybe run herself a hot bath, light some candles, and soak for an hour or so. Well, she might as well take such moments before things like that became too difficult. She couldn't imagine many candlelit baths after the baby arrived.

She entered the house and listened for signs of life. Edward had been due to meet a client in the mid-afternoon, but he'd promised to be back by five, in time to start the evening meal. 'Edward, are you home?'

No answer.

She entered the living room. All was quiet. And no sign of him in the kitchen, either. The meeting must have run late.

But when she got to the bedroom, she saw the one-line note, lying on top of the covers.

Sorry for everything. This is for the best. Goodbye.

'No, you can't have . . .'

But, a few seconds later, her fears were confirmed. A check of the wardrobe revealed that his overnight bags had gone.

Emma had returned to the flat as quickly as she could, straight from the deli. Although she still felt relatively safe among the London crowds, and there was no reason to think that this person would be physically threatening, the thought that he might be watching her, toying with her, was completely unnerving.

Buying the meal. It was designed to unsettle me.

She just wanted to disappear out of sight. She spent the afternoon on the sofa, watching television, wondering whether to call Dan and tell him what had happened. She decided to wait until he got home from work.

She hid the letter that Charlotte had given her in the bottom of her sock drawer, unsure whether she would ever open it.

At around five Lizzy phoned, and she told her everything, including what Charlotte had said and given to her, as well as the mysterious person who had paid for their meal. Lizzy offered to come over, but Emma knew Dan would be back within the hour.

It was an hour that went by very slowly.

Emma waited until they had eaten before telling Dan about what had happened at the café. He was washing up as she was sitting at the kitchen table, flicking through the latest copy of *Red* magazine, wondering how to tell him.

In the end, she just blurted it out. 'I think the person was following me today.'

Dan was rinsing a cup, but the shock stopped him dead. 'What! Why didn't you tell me earlier?'

'I didn't want to spoil dinner.'

He put down the cup and tea towel. 'Em . . .'

'I know, it sounds ridiculous,' she acknowledged. But maybe it was just her attempt to snatch a bit of normality and happiness. The meal had been lovely, even with the thoughts of what had happened weighing heavily on her mind.

Dan moved over to the table. 'What the hell happened?'

'Not a lot, really. It was like in Cornwall – all mysterious. Lizzy and I had lunch in a café, in Soho, and when I went to pay, someone else had already settled the bill.'

Dan looked horrified. 'It was him?'

'I think so. At least, I assume that it must be the same person. It was definitely a man.'

'And you didn't see anyone in there?'

'No. At one point, earlier on, we'd looked around, and there definitely wasn't anyone there who looked like Stephen Myers. But I was in the café for a while, and later I didn't really notice who else had come in.'

'How do you know it was a man?'

'The waitress told me.'

'Of course,' Dan said, distracted by his thoughts. He looked at her. 'And you didn't see anything else afterwards? No one following you?'

'No. I came straight back here, as quickly as I could. I did keep an eye out, but I didn't see anyone.'

'Thank God Lizzy was with you.'

'She wasn't then,' Emma admitted. 'She had to go for a meeting at the theatre.'

He was surprised. 'You were in there on your own?'

'No. I was with Charlotte Harris – Stuart's sister.'

'Stuart Harris's sister? I don't understand.'

Emma told him everything that had happened. He listened carefully, shaking his head at several points when she outlined what Charlotte had accused her of. She didn't mention the package that Charlotte had given to her. She still feared what it might contain, and if she was ever going to tell Dan about it, she would need to know what was in it first.

'I can't believe she was so nasty to you,' Dan said, when she had finished relaying the story. 'I mean, she can't blame you for what happened to Stuart.'

'She can, and she does,' Emma said.

'I know she *does* blame you, but what I mean is, it wasn't your fault. None of it was your fault.'

'I know. But she's grieving, Dan. And that's making her lash out.'

'It's no excuse to attack you.'

'She's angry that I didn't attend the funeral. I think that's the real problem. When I didn't go, she interpreted it as meaning that I didn't care about Stuart, or the fact that he was dead. But that wasn't the reason why I stayed away.'

'You could have gone, you know. I wouldn't have minded.'

Emma wasn't sure that he meant it, but it was sweet of him to pretend. 'I was mindful about how it might affect you, of course,' she admitted. 'But it wasn't just that. Charlotte might have wanted me to be there, but I just thought it would be a bad idea. I didn't want attention on me. And I didn't want to run into his girlfriend. It wasn't my place to be there.'

'For what it's worth, I think you made the right decision,' Dan said.

She smiled. 'Thank you. It's worth a lot.'

He tapped the table and whistled through his teeth. 'Today wasn't a good day, was it?'

'Not really, no.'

'Come here,' he said, pulling her close. 'I just wish we knew who the hell this person is. If I could just get my hands on him . . .'

'You know what trouble that sort of vigilantism got my dad into.'

'I know. I don't really mean it. But, Em, I really feel that this person, whoever they are, is such a coward. I mean, what he did with the flowers, in the toilet at the theatre and now today, paying for the meal – it *is* cowardly, really. Staying in the shadows like that, stalking around in the darkness.'

'Well, I hope he is a coward. Because it would mean, I hope, that he'd keep his distance.'

'True.'

'Do you think it's worth telling the police about what happened today?'

'I think we should, first thing tomorrow. Although I doubt it will make any difference to what they'll say. Don't worry, Em,' he added, noticing her dejection. 'We'll get through this.'

'I know we will.'

Dan went back to washing up, while Emma read some more of her magazine.

'I was thinking,' Dan said, topping up the water. 'How about we get away from London tomorrow, you and me? Just get out of the city for the day?'

Emma looked up from the magazine. 'Where to?'

'I was thinking Windsor. We've been meaning to go there for ages, and it's not actually that far – a direct train from Waterloo. We could visit the castle, and they do tours of Eton College. We can check online to see if we have to book in advance.'

Emma smiled. 'Sounds good. I've not been there since I was ten years old.'

'Might as well do something good while I've got the day off. The weather forecast is sunny, so we could also walk through the park in front of the castle. Go somewhere in the town for a bite to eat, maybe buy some royal souvenirs.' He smiled knowingly. Dan was fully aware that Emma was a keen royalist, and loved visiting such places and collecting books and trinkets relating to the royal family. They'd been on the tour of Buckingham Palace the previous year, and during a short trip to Edinburgh had visited the Palace of Holyroodhouse.

'It's a great idea,' she said. 'Really great. Just what I need – especially after today.'

Later on, curled up on the sofa watching television while Dan took a shower, Emma thought about what he had said about the cowardliness of the person: keeping that bit of distance – too far to be too threatening, but close enough to unsettle. It reminded her of someone.

It reminded her of the man who had waited outside the studio gates in the pouring rain, approached her with the scruffy notepad and pencil and spent the early hours of the morning outside her flat, like a prowling cat.

This person is just like Stephen Myers.

19

He slid down into his chair and booted up the computer. The email was waiting for him. He read the message which was, as usual, professional and to the point. Then he opened the attachment and scrutinised the contents.

'Interesting . . .'

He hit the print button and then stood up, getting a bottle of Bud from the fridge. Gulping down a mouthful, he retrieved the printout and flopped down on the sofa, his feet up on the table. He finished the bottle in three big glugs, which was just long enough to read the papers as carefully as he needed to.

He smiled. 'I like this a lot.'

He got back in front of the computer and typed out a reply. He kept it short, but made sure that everything was there. Hitting send, he opened his photo folder and began clicking through the images from his sojourn to Cornwall. He stopped at an image of Emma Holden on the beach, hand in hand with Dan Carlton.

Do I really feel jealous?

He smiled, moving on to a shot of the couple coming out of the vineyard. He zoomed in on Emma so that it was cutting out Dan, who was walking a few steps behind her.

I do! I'm feeling jealous!

He grinned broadly, impressed by his own abilities.

Surely no one can deny me my opportunity now. Not after the past few days.

He reached across and grabbed a sketch pad and pencil from the nearby bookcase. In the middle of the pad was a sketch portrait of Emma. He had taken great inspiration from it. He looked at it each morning and evening, just gazing into her eyes. Maybe that had been the key factor in his success. He was very pleased with the image.

He must be so close now to achieving his goal. How could he seal the deal?

'That's it!'

It was crazy, but was just perfect for the circumstances. The only question was, would somewhere be open at this time of night?

He went online and found a place in less than a couple of minutes. It was only just down the road, and was open throughout the night.

He called the number and was delighted to find that they could accommodate his request. If he went straight down, they would do it there and then.

He sat back and smiled, still marvelling at his inspired idea.

'Maybe David Sherborn saw the person in the café,' Dan said, as they sat together on the sofa.

'He definitely wasn't in the café,' Emma replied. 'But I guess he might have seen him, if he was following before or after I went in there.'

'You don't think it's worth calling him to ask?'

Emma consulted her watch. Half past ten. 'Not tonight. If he sees anything significant, I'm sure he will get in touch with me. Although I do need to text him,' she said, remembering that he would be waiting for tomorrow's instructions. 'I need to let him know about Windsor.'

She tapped a short message into her mobile, stating their destination and time of departure from Waterloo, and pressed send. 'If we decide to get a different train, I'll let him know.'

Dan looked uncomfortable. 'It feels weird, outlining your every move to some stranger, so he can follow you.'

'He's not quite a stranger. And it *is* for a good reason.'

'I know, I know. It was a good idea of Lizzy's. I was a bit reluctant about it at first, but now I've come around to it.'

Emma was surprised by that. 'But you didn't say you had reservations at the time.' It wasn't like Dan to be shy with his views.

'You were all so enthusiastic and, to be honest, I couldn't think of anything better. So I just went along with it. And I'm glad I did. I just hope he comes up with the goods.'

'So do I. He's our only option at the moment.'

'Thinking about it,' Dan continued, 'I suppose we can't expect the police to do much, really. I mean, from their perspective, the real danger – Peter Myers – is safely behind bars. But I still thought they'd treat it more seriously than like it's just some minor nuisance.'

'I guess that's all it is, at the moment. Maybe if there had been threats, they'd react differently,' Emma ventured.

'Probably. But the incident in the theatre toilets, if that was the same person, well, I'd say that was pretty damn threatening.'

'You're right,' Emma said. 'It was really intimidating.'

'You really didn't see him following you today? David Sherborn, I mean.'

'No, not at all. Maybe he wasn't following us.'

'He said he would, though.'

'Yes, in his studio he said he'd start almost straight away.'

'Then he might have seen something.'

Just then the phone rang. Its shrill cry shocked them both, coming at this relatively late hour.

'I'll get it,' Dan said, moving out into the hallway.

Emma waited pensively. She had a thing about phone calls late at night: she always expected them to herald bad news.

'Miranda? Are you okay?'

Dan's concerned tone brought Emma hurrying out into the hallway. 'Not the baby?' she asked in horror.

Dan shook his head. 'No, he's not here, I'm really sorry. Emma's right next to me. Would you like me to put her on?' He brought the receiver down and placed a hand over the microphone. 'It's your dad. He's gone AWOL,' he whispered. 'Just upped and left in the car.'

135

'What?' She took the phone, struggling to believe what Dan had just told her.

Surely Dad wouldn't abandon Miranda and the baby just like that?

'Are you okay?' Dan said, entering the bedroom. Emma was lying on top of the covers, staring at the ceiling. 'Want to talk?'

'I can't believe he'd do this,' Emma said. 'To Miranda or to me. Just walk away without explanation. He's so selfish.'

Dan sat down on the bed and put his arms around her.

She sat up, hugging a pillow. 'I mean, she's beside herself with worry, and he's not answering his phone.'

It was eleven o'clock – half an hour after Miranda had called to tell them the news about Edward. Miranda had rung primarily to check that he hadn't gone round to their flat, more out of hope than expectation.

'You know,' Emma said, 'I thought he'd learnt his lesson after what happened a few weeks ago. But he hasn't changed. He hasn't changed at all.'

'He's under a lot of pressure,' Dan said. 'It's not an excuse for running off, but maybe he just had to get away for a bit.'

Emma shook her head. 'The trouble with my dad is that he won't talk to anyone. He doesn't even let his nearest family get close enough to understand how he's feeling.' She shrugged. 'He wasn't always like that. Before Mum got ill, he wasn't like that at all. He was open, caring. He was never the same after she died. The Dad I used to know would never have done the kinds of things he's done in the past few weeks.'

'Events can change us,' Dan said.

Emma didn't really hear that remark. 'Maybe I should go over to their house. Miranda must be going out of her mind with worry. She shouldn't be put under so much stress, with the baby . . .'

'You did offer to go over. She said she was okay.'

'I know, but she probably didn't want to put me out.'

'Possibly. Or she might just want some space.'

Emma nodded. 'I'll try his phone again.' She keyed in the number.

She had called multiple times since hearing the news, each time without success and with increasing worry and frustration. But she would keep trying until she got an answer. Emma had also called Will to let him know the news. He hadn't heard from their dad, either.

The call cut straight through to the answer service, just like all the other times. She had already left three messages, so this time she just clicked off. 'It's still switched off,' she said, spinning the phone onto the bed.

'Maybe you'll have better luck in the morning,' Dan offered. 'He's probably checked into a hotel. Give him a night to think things over and he'll no doubt be in touch tomorrow, to explain what's going on. I can't see him leaving you all hanging like that. Whatever your dad might have done in the past, he would never want you, Will or Miranda to suffer. He's always done things with the best of intentions, even if he's misguided sometimes.'

'Maybe,' Emma replied, not particularly believing it. There had been a time when she had felt she had known her father, but not now – not after the revelations of how he had kept Stephen Myers' death a secret, and how he had nearly killed Peter Myers with that gun. He might come back and get in touch, but it was equally possible that her father intended the break to be permanent. He could be on the road, getting as far away from them all as possible, driving without any particular destination in mind.

She had an unsettling feeling that he might just disappear for ever, leaving his old life, with all its worries, far behind.

20

Despite everything that was happening, Dan and Emma enjoyed their day in Windsor. During the first couple of hours, Emma did keep half an eye out for the Stephen Myers impersonator, and she also wondered whether David Sherborn had travelled with them. But, after that, she forgot about her troubles and just had a good time. The only break in the enjoyment was a call to Miranda at lunch, to check whether her dad had been in touch.

He still hadn't.

Even that didn't dent their happiness. Maybe it was because they were both so determined to end their holiday period on a positive note.

'Thank you,' Emma said, as they walked out of the castle and down through the impressive grounds. The sun was shining and it felt great. 'This is like being back on holiday.'

'It is,' Dan agreed.

Emma turned to look at him, and he brushed a stray hair away from her face. 'When we're alone, everything feels right.'

'I know. Sometimes it's a pity that we can't shut out the world.' He kissed her warmly.

One hundred metres away, their kiss was captured with a telephoto lens.

Followed by another click from a different direction.

'Impressed?' Lizzy arrived at the flat right on time. It was early on Wednesday morning, just before nine, the day Emma had arranged to meet the agent Diana Saunders. It was also Dan's first proper day back in the office – he had an important team meeting about a new international client, so Lizzy had offered to accompany Emma to her meeting. After what had happened at the deli café, where someone had obviously been watching her, they all thought it was increasingly important that Emma shouldn't be alone.

'Come in,' Emma said. 'Dan's just left.'

As Emma boiled the kettle, Lizzy jumped right in. 'Have you told him about the letter from Stuart?'

Emma dropped two tea bags into the pot and poured on the boiling water. 'No, not yet.' She wasn't certain that she was ever going to tell Dan about the letter from Stuart Harris. 'I'm still not sure that I'm actually going to read it.' Since her meeting with Charlotte, the letter had remained buried in her sock drawer.

Lizzy let the subject drop. 'Did you have a nice day yesterday?'

Emma beamed. 'Really good, under the circumstances. We went inside Windsor Castle, and saw some of the Crown Jewels that are on display there at the moment. They were amazing. We also toured Eton College, which was pretty cool. It's a totally different world, you know, Lizzy.'

'I bet. A bit different to the comprehensive I went to.'

'And me.'

'Sounds like the day was just what the doctor ordered,' Lizzy said. 'You look much happier than you did on Monday.'

Emma poured the tea. 'Thanks, I am a lot more positive. I think what yesterday did is help me to put things in perspective. I mean, it was horrible what happened at the weekend, but I sense this is just someone getting a kick out of frightening us. Dan said this person is a coward, and he's right, Lizzy. They stay out of sight because they're a coward.'

'Sounds a bit like—' Lizzy cut herself off, deciding that it wouldn't be wise to say what she was about to say.

Emma brought the two cups of tea over and placed them on

the table. 'I know what you're thinking. That it sounds like Stephen Myers.'

Lizzy kept quiet.

'I had the same thought, on Monday evening.'

'Maybe they're a good impersonator,' Lizzy said.

'Maybe.' Emma hadn't thought of it that way before, but now Lizzy said it, it made perfect sense. This person was impersonating Stephen Myers physically and in personality.

Unless it is really Stephen Myers after all.

Emma shook off that thought. She took a sip of the tea, and wondered how Miranda was. They'd called her during the day while they were in Windsor, and again when they returned home – partly to check that she was okay, but also in the hope that her father might have made contact.

Lizzy seemed to read Emma's mind. 'No word from your dad?'

Emma shook her head. 'Nothing. I'm ringing Miranda, to check she's okay and to see whether he's been in touch.'

'How's she coping with it all?'

Emma screwed up her face. 'I suspect not very well, judging by how she sounds on the phone. But she said she's okay. Maybe she doesn't feel comfortable opening up to me, because we're not that close.' Emma and Miranda had had a difficult relationship, which, although never hostile, had been on the cool side. Things were getting warmer between them, however, since the announcement that Miranda was pregnant. But Emma could understand if Miranda didn't want to talk to her about her innermost feelings.

'And no news from David Sherborn?'

'No. Nothing.' They were due to meet with him later that day, to see whether he had managed to identify anyone who was following her. Emma now doubted whether he would come up with anything. 'To be honest, I'm starting to wonder whether he's actually been doing what he promised.'

'Really?'

'Well, I haven't heard from him or seen him at all since our meeting on Monday. And he's not replied to the texts I sent, letting him know where I was.'

'I guess he didn't really need to reply. He just needed to read your text and go to that location.'

Emma shrugged. 'I would have thought I'd see him, maybe not a lot, but occasionally. For instance, yesterday in Windsor, I looked around quite a bit, particularly in the morning, but there was no sign of him.'

'Maybe he's got better at staying out of sight.'

'Yeah – maybe I'm underestimating him.'

Emma and Lizzy got off the tube at Piccadilly Circus, glad to be out in the relatively fresher air at street level – the underground network was a great thing, but it could really do with air-conditioning, especially during warmer spells.

The agency was situated just a few minutes from the station, in the heart of the capital. This was prime real-estate territory, and rent on the two-storey, glass-fronted building that housed the EXCEL-ENT media agency must have been astronomical. The agency was just a few years old, having been set up by a breakaway group of agents from a traditional agency, following a fallout over company direction in the new digital age. It had a reputation for maximising opportunities and income for their clients, and it covered all fields of media, including publishing, television, film, music and digital. The agency now represented some of the biggest stars in the entertainment industry.

That was why it had seemed such an honour to receive the unsolicited invitation from Diana Saunders. She was a company director, and one of the founding members. She was also leading new developments with the company. From what Emma had heard, most of Diana's working week was now spent flying between the UK and the United States, where the agency had just set up a New York office. So the fact she was prepared to take time to meet with Emma felt like a huge compliment.

'Well,' Lizzy said, looking up at the building, 'good luck. Just give me a call when you're finished. I'll be in the swanky, too-expensive-for-me clothes shops just around the corner. I might try a few things on, you know, private fashion show – try but no buy.' She smiled mischievously.

Emma's mind was on the meeting, so she didn't really take in Lizzy's joke. 'Sounds good.'

'It'll be fine,' Lizzy said, noticing that she was worried. 'Just remember, no matter how bullish this Diana Saunders is, she wants *you*, so you've got nothing to lose. In fact, she should be nervous, not you.'

'I bet she isn't, though. I don't think people like Diana Saunders ever get nervous.'

Despite Lizzy's comforting words, Emma's nerves were taut as she reported to Reception. This was all so different to what she was used to – her long-standing former agent had worked from home, not a gleaming corporate office.

She was directed to a waiting lift. It rose smoothly, barely perceptibly, and she emerged into an open-plan office, where there were dozens of people, mostly young, hunched over computers. Some were on the telephone.

A young, beautifully coiffured girl in her early twenties approached and proffered a hand, smiling broadly. Emma wondered whether she was an intern. 'Emma, pleased to meet you. I'm Catharine, Diana's assistant. She'll be with you in a minute. She's just finishing a call. Please, just take a seat through there.' She gestured towards a glass-panelled office to the left. 'Can I get you a tea, coffee?'

'Just water would be great.'

'Sure.'

Emma perched on the edge of a chair in the office as Catharine returned with the water. 'Here you are.' Instead of just bringing a glass, she had a full bottle. It was a French brand that Emma hadn't heard of before. It looked expensive. Catharine filled the glass, which also contained a slice of lemon, and left the bottle on the glass table. Another glass was filled and left next to it. 'Diana will be with you shortly.'

Emma was sipping the water as Diana breezed into the room.

'Emma, how *wonderful* to meet you! Diana Saunders,' she said, offering her hand. 'Sorry for the wait.' She flipped her trademark dark-rimmed glasses up into her hairline. She was wearing a dark, 1980s-style power suit, and her jet-black hair was pulled tightly back. She pulled up a chair and took a drink from the second glass. 'Important call from a publisher in New York. I'm expecting to confirm a six-figure deal for one of our exciting, up-and-coming authors by lunchtime. We've got a rather tasty transatlantic auction going on, but these guys are ready to make a game-changing offer that will, frankly, blow the others out of the water.' She smiled triumphantly. 'You can tell someone is desperate to close the deal when they call you at five in the morning, their time.'

Emma didn't quite know what to say to that. 'It's really nice to meet you, too,' she managed. She felt somewhat in awe of this woman, of whom she'd heard so much.

'Yes, yes, that's great, Emma,' Diana said, distracted. She had pulled out her mobile phone and was scrolling through the display. 'I have an email here, somewhere. Somewhere . . . yes, here it is.' She placed the phone on the desk without any explanation.

Emma smiled, not quite knowing what to say next. 'I was surprised when you got in touch.'

'Good, good!' Diana nodded. 'I like to surprise people. Tell me, Emma, what's the most captivating plot you've been involved in so far?' She replaced her glasses and sat back.

'Well, er . . .' This was an unexpected first question. Emma tried to think through some of the many plots that had occurred during her time on *Up My Street*. Okay, they were often outlandish, but they were nearly always captivating. Some people viewed soaps as a low form of entertainment, but to her mind they were one of the cleverest and most technically adept forms, knowing just how to draw people in and keep their attention on what happened next – which was why millions of viewers tuned in to every episode. 'Maybe the episode in the soap I was in, with the fire in the nightclub,' she said. That had been one of the most expensive episodes in the show's history, and Emma had played a starring role. She was very proud of that one.

'Wrong!' Diana said. 'Absolutely, totally *wrong*.'

Emma flushed red. 'I don't underst—'

'Your real life,' Diana said. '*That's* the most captivating plot.'

'But . . . I thought you meant . . .'

'Fiction?' Diana raised an eyebrow. 'Fact, fiction, it's all the same to me.'

'I'm sorry, I *really* don't understand.'

Diana picked up the mobile phone. 'Have you heard of Firework Films?'

Emma shook her head.

'They're a young, vibrant production company. Ambitious, boundary-pushers – the kind of people I like to work with. They specialise in gritty, edgy programming that grabs you by the throat and refuses to let go. You've no doubt seen some of their work – *The Shortest Girl on Earth, Married to my Pet, Life of a Junkie, Skidrow Rehab*.'

Warning bells sounded. Emma had certainly heard of these programmes; every one of them had made headlines because of their controversial topics and the voyeuristic – some argued, exploitative – approach taken by the makers. To Emma, it was reality TV at its very worst: a freak show for the twenty-first century.

She maintained a neutral expression as she crafted a careful response. 'I've heard of them, yes.'

If Emma was revealing her disquiet at the thought of the company, Diana didn't pick up on it. 'Good. Well, they have an offer for you. An offer I'm sure you'll agree represents a fantastic opportunity.' She waited for a reaction.

'What kind of opportunity?' Emma felt ill.

Surely something dreamt up by Firework Films isn't going to appeal . . .

'They want to produce a docudrama of what happened to you, Emma. The drama would feature actors playing the parts of you, your family and others. But they would also want to feature cut-away mini-interviews with the real players in the plot, including you, of course. As such, it would be a complementary mix of approaches, giving the viewer a real insight into what happened. I think it would be dynamite.'

Now Emma had no hesitation in vocalising her thoughts. 'No,' she said, in an instinctive reaction. 'I'm not interested.'

She couldn't believe what she was hearing. So this was why the great Diana Saunders had called her in – she wasn't interested in working to further her career; she simply thought there was a done deal she could persuade Emma to take.

Diana looked unmoved, as if she hadn't even computed Emma's response. 'And depending on the ratings, they would then like to make another show, focusing on your return to acting. They would accompany you on your journey as you seek to make it big.'

Emma nearly laughed with disbelief, but actually she felt incredibly angry. Her life and the lives of her friends and family were being touted as cheap, throwaway entertainment. All that pain and anguish, the deaths, the fear – that was to be served up to satisfy viewers? No way would she ever be a part of it.

She decided to test Diana's motives. 'What would you say if I turned this down? Would you still be interested in taking me on as a client?'

Diana laughed at what she thought at first was a joke. But when the reality dawned, she was shocked. 'You're seriously considering turning this down?'

'Would you still take me on as a client if I did?'

Diana's hesitation confirmed what Emma already thought. 'In all seriousness, I think you'd be absolutely crazy to walk away from this golden opportunity.'

'Yes, yes, I am.'

'Then you're a fool.'

Emma stood up. 'I think I'd better go.'

Diana realised she had overstepped the mark. She rose from her chair and held up her hands by way of an apology, in the hope of convincing Emma to not walk straight out of the door. 'I'm sorry, Emma, what I meant to say is that it would be foolish to let this slip through your fingers. I'm really passionate about this project, and I don't want you to make any rash decisions.'

'I'm sorry,' Emma replied. 'It really doesn't interest me.'

Diana's face hardened. Clearly she wasn't used to rejection. 'Do you really think you've got a future in acting?'

Her sudden, abrasive tone stopped Emma dead.

Diana smiled cruelly. 'You turned down the biggest opportunity in your life a few weeks ago. And by pulling out you caused a lot of problems for the people making that movie. Everyone in the business knows now that you can't rely on Emma Holden. She may just walk away, decide that she doesn't want to do it any more, and to hell with the consequences. Do you *really* think there will be people queuing up to employ you?'

'If it means not having to work with people like you, then I really don't care,' Emma replied, exiting the office and heading straight for the lift.

Diana Saunders didn't follow.

Emma swept out of the building and walked a few paces down the street. She leant back on the wall of a neighbouring building, trying to control her breathing. That had been one of the worst experiences of her career. But at least she had stood up to that woman, and it felt good. She called Lizzy, who arrived within minutes.

Just as Emma was in the middle of explaining the situation, her mobile rang.

'Emma, it's David Sherborn.'

'Oh, hi, are you still okay for meeting later?'

'Sure am. In fact, we can meet earlier if you like.'

'Fine by me, I'm out with Lizzy at the moment. We're . . .'

'In a side street just off Piccadilly Circus.'

Emma looked around. She suddenly spotted him off towards their left, next to a postbox. He held up a hand. She smiled, despite herself. 'Now, then?'

'Perfect,' he said. 'I've got something really interesting to show you.'

Part Three

21

Diana Saunders slammed shut the door to her office so hard the internal walls shook, sending a book toppling off a shelf and crashing onto her desk. She had never been so angry.

How could that girl refuse me?

She paced around the room in a fury. The door opened and Catharine started to come in.

'Out!' Diana shouted.

Catharine looked shocked. She backed out. 'Sorry, Diana, sorry.'

Diana threw her hands up into the air. 'No one rejects me!'

This is the last time I do a favour for a friend.

She stood at the office window, hands on hips. 'You *stupid* girl.'

When she had calmed down sufficiently, she called the number. 'The answer was no,' she said, moderating her voice so as to appear calm. She preferred not to show her emotions to external clients – even those whom she considered friends. It was a sign of weakness. 'Emma Holden rejected the opportunity that was presented to her, and walked out. *No one* has ever walked out on me like that . . . Well, she was very clear about it. Actually, I was impressed by the strength of her opinion, even though I think she's making another huge mistake . . . Just don't ask me to have any more dealings with that girl. I did what you asked, and that's the end of it.'

She ended the call and gazed out again at the London street. There was a timid knock on the door. 'Come in,' she said without turning round.

It was Catharine again. 'Really sorry to interrupt, Diana,' she said to Diana's back, her voice quivering. 'Donaldson and

Donaldson are on the phone again from New York. They want to speak to you.'

That brightened her mood. The smell of victory was growing ever stronger. Now it was time to make them sweat. 'Tell them I'm in a meeting. I'll call them back this afternoon.'

'Let me get those,' David said as they ordered their coffees in the Starbucks that was just round the corner. Emma and Lizzy took their drinks to a free table and David joined them shortly afterwards, pulling a brown envelope from his jacket pocket as he sat down. He placed it on the table, without explanation.

'So,' Emma said, as they all looked at one another. 'Have you got some news?'

'I have,' David said. He sat back in his chair and took a sip of his coffee. 'I've got to admit, I was really hesitant about doing this when you first asked me. But, to be honest, I've really enjoyed the past few days. Maybe I should look to change career, and go into surveillance full time.'

Emma and Lizzy smiled politely, but wanted to find out what he knew. Having convinced herself that he wouldn't come up with anything, Emma's hopes had now risen dramatically.

He seemed to sense their impatience, and pulled out a photograph from the envelope, laying it on the table. He placed a finger on the image. 'This guy I spotted pretty much straight away. Monday, in fact, shortly after I started to follow you – he was pretty obvious.'

Emma was disappointed. 'Adrian Spencer.'

David was surprised. 'You know him?'

'He's a reporter for the *Daily Post*,' Lizzy explained. 'For the past few weeks he's been pestering us for quotes about what happened. He's writing a feature article on Dan's kidnapping.'

'Right. Well, this guy was definitely following you for quite some time on Monday.'

Emma pondered. *Could Adrian Spencer be the person who followed us down to Cornwall?* But she quickly dismissed that possibility – he didn't remotely resemble Stephen Myers and, anyway, Lizzy had met him in the capital on the very weekend they were on holiday, so he couldn't have been down there.

David Sherborn continued. 'I also saw him taking photographs, and making notes.'

Photographs? Emma wanted to speak to Adrian Spencer about that. What was he intending to do with them – use them with his feature story? That just wasn't on. Then she had a thought.

'Were you following us when we were in Soho, at the deli café?'

'Yes, I was.'

'Did you see anyone go in there, that may have been following us?'

'No, sorry, I didn't. But I've got to admit, you were in there for so long, I did go off and have a coffee. Why?'

'It's just that someone in there paid for our meals. I thought you might have seen who it was . . .' Something occurred to her. 'Maybe it was Adrian Spencer.' *But why?*

'Well, I definitely didn't see him following you around then. He stopped when you were in John Lewis.'

'Was he following me in Windsor yesterday?'

'Only for the first part of the morning,' David Sherborn replied. 'I didn't see him after eleven, eleven thirty.'

'So you *were* in Windsor?'

He smiled. 'Oh, yes. The security services are probably investigating me as I speak, given that I was waiting outside Windsor castle for two hours with a telephoto lens while you were on your guided tour.'

'Sorry,' Emma said, feeling sorry for him having to hang around for so long – it wasn't as if he was being paid for the inconvenience. 'We *were* in there for a long time.'

'It's okay. At least it wasn't raining.' He grinned.

'I guess you had a quiet day then,' Lizzy said, 'if Adrian Spencer disappeared early on.'

'Oh, I wouldn't say that.' David cocked a meaningful eyebrow at them.

Emma was intrigued. 'What do you mean?'

'Well, Adrian Spencer might not have been around for long, but *this* guy was.' He placed a second photograph over the first. 'I noticed him first of all at Waterloo Station. He was hanging back, but I spotted him. Somehow I just noticed that he was following you, even though it wasn't that obvious. He caught the same train. Do you recognise him?'

Emma scrutinised the image, Lizzy at her shoulder doing the same. The man, probably in his mid-twenties, had a look of Stephen Myers, although he was much better looking. His face was thin, the same as Myers, and his nose was prominent. His hair was dark, again matching her one-time stalker. One thing was clear, though: this person may have had a likeness of Stephen Myers, particularly from a distance, but it definitely was not him.

That alone was a big relief.

'No.' Emma shook her head.

Is this the person who followed us to Cornwall? He certainly matches the description given by the assistant at the florist's.

'He wasn't in the same carriage as you. I was sitting facing him, but some way down, because I didn't want to risk arousing any suspicion. He spent most of the journey on his phone, or reading through some paperwork. When we arrived, I hung back a little, and followed him, as he followed you.'

'I didn't see anyone,' Emma said. 'I was looking, but I didn't see either you or him.' She thought she had done a good job of scanning the area, but it seemed not.

David didn't look at all surprised. 'He was careful not to be seen by you. As I said, he was hanging back, staying out of view. He had a telephoto lens on his camera, which he used quite a lot.'

'I don't understand all this,' Emma said. 'Who this person is, why he's doing what he's doing . . .'

David brought out a third photograph. 'He also followed you into the castle, and around the town. He ate in the same restaurant as you.'

Emma shuddered at the thought.

'He then tailed you down to Eton College, but didn't go in. Later, he picked you up again as you were walking in the grounds outside the castle. I got this snap of him, photographing you from a distance.' He showed them the image of the man, the camera with the big lens raised to his face. He chuckled to himself. 'This guy had no idea that at that very moment he was being photographed, too.'

Emma could see the irony, but she didn't feel like laughing. 'What happened next?'

'That's when he stopped following you. He caught the next train back to Waterloo.'

Emma was surprised. 'You followed him back to London?'

He nodded. 'I know you said I only had to follow you, but I guess I got caught up in it all, and wanted to find out more about this guy. So I thought I might as well see where he was going.'

Emma sensed David was building up to something big.

So too did Lizzy. She leant forward in anticipation. 'So where did he go?'

David Sherborn smiled. 'That's where it gets really interesting.' He brought out a final photograph.

Emma couldn't believe it. The man who had followed them in Windsor was standing at the doorstep of a house.

And he was talking to a man they knew only too well.

22

'*Guy Roberts*? He went to meet Guy Roberts?' Emma couldn't believe it. Hadn't that unscrupulous casting director caused enough trouble for them already?

How is he involved in all of this?

David nodded. 'Our mystery man went straight round to his house, right from the station. It looks like he's up to his old tricks again.' Lizzy noticed he had the grace to look faintly embarrassed – after all, it wasn't so long since he'd been doing the same thing himself for Guy Roberts.

Emma was struggling to understand what the connection could possibly be. 'Did he go in to Guy's house?'

'No. He didn't get past the door.'

Emma needed to know more. 'You couldn't hear what was being said?'

'Too far away, sorry. I couldn't risk getting too close.'

'Did they look like they were friends?'

He shrugged. 'I really can't say. They were only talking for a short time. No more than a couple of minutes. They weren't arguing, I can say that. But on the other hand, they weren't laughing and joking, either.'

'Where did the man go after he left Guy Roberts?'

'I stopped following him at that point. Sorry, I had to get home.'

'Of course,' Emma said, trying to hide her disappointment. She felt frustrated at being left with these tantalising pieces of information, but she understood that David had been limited in what he could find out. He'd already gone above and beyond what had been asked of him. 'Thanks for doing this, I really appreciate it.'

'No problem at all,' he said. 'I just wish I could have found out more for you.'

'So, are we going to see him?' Lizzy said outside the coffee shop, as they parted company with David Sherborn. He'd offered to help more if needed, but had reiterated that the rest of his week was filled with client bookings.

'Sorry?' Emma was lost in thought.

What does all this have to do with Guy Roberts? Why has he sent someone to follow me again?

'Guy Roberts,' Lizzy said. 'I say we go straight round to his house, and have it out with him. You know, confront him with what we know, and demand that he tells us who this person is. And what the hell is going on.'

Emma looked at Lizzy. 'So you think Guy Roberts is behind this again?'

Lizzy nodded, emphatically. 'He must be! Look at the evidence! And we know what he's like.'

Emma nodded thoughtfully. 'Still, I don't think we should jump to conclusions. Guy Roberts must know a lot of people. I'm going to try and keep an open mind until we know more.' She thought some more. It could be risky rushing into a situation in which they had only partial information. It could actually be counterproductive – she had the feeling that Guy Roberts, if not approached carefully this time, would just put up barriers rather than be helpful. After all, he would surely not jump at helping Emma, after she had rejected him for the film role. 'I just think we need to think about this, before rushing in making accusations.'

Lizzy looked unconvinced, and disappointed. But she didn't look like she was going to argue. 'So,' she said, after a few moments of contemplation, 'if we aren't going to do that, then what should we do?'

'First of all, I want to speak to Adrian Spencer's boss.'

Lizzy sparked to life. 'The *Daily Post*?'

Emma nodded. 'They've got to be told what he's doing. It's not right, following us around like that, taking photographs. If we get him off our backs, it will be one less thing to worry about.'

'They might know about what he's doing. They might have sanctioned it.'

'Maybe. But whatever the case, I want to let them know that we're not putting up with it any longer.'

Before setting off for the *Daily Post* headquarters, Emma called Dan to let him know about everything that had happened. She was a little uncertain about disturbing him at work, but he needed to know.

'Em. How did the meeting go?' he said.

Emma had to take a moment to think about to what he was referring. It seemed so long ago, so unimportant, in the light of what David had told them. 'Terrible. Diana Saunders was only interested in representing me if I agreed to cooperate with a production company who want to make a docudrama about your kidnapping.'

'You're kidding me.'

'Honestly. I told her no way, which of course she didn't like. I just walked out.'

'Good for you. I can't believe that it was all about setting you up for something like that. You did say, though, that you weren't sure of her – your instincts were obviously right.'

'I know. It's disappointing in a way, and it was pretty uncomfortable. But I'm fine.'

'Good.'

'Something else has happened, though.'

'Oh?'

'David Sherborn has come up with some useful information – he's identified the person who's been following me. They followed us in Windsor.'

There was a moment's silence, then Dan said, 'Well, that's good news, isn't it? Who is it, and how the hell did he know we were going to Windsor?'

'I don't know. Either he followed us from the flat, or someone told him we were going.'

Emma heard Dan exhale.

Just then a bus appeared and they stepped on. Downstairs was only a quarter full and they took a seat just down from the middle doors.

'He showed us photographs of the person,' Emma said, as she settled into her seat. 'He had a bit of a resemblance to Stephen Myers, although it wasn't him, thank God. I don't recognise him.'

'That's a shame. But at least we've got more information that we can take to the police.'

'There's more. David followed him back from Windsor. The man went straight round to Guy Roberts' house.'

'You're joking.' Dan's surprise was obvious.

'David's got the evidence in the photos.'

'But what's he got to do with this?'

'No idea. But he knows the person who's following me.'

'You said he had a resemblance to Stephen Myers?'

'He's got a similar build, and the same thin face and pointy nose. The hair colour's similar, too. He doesn't *really* look like Stephen Myers but, at a distance, wearing the right clothes, he could be mistaken for him.'

'And if he had his hair arranged differently,' Dan was thinking out loud. 'Or was wearing a wig . . .'

'Maybe, yes.'

There was a pause. 'So, what are you up to now?'

She hesitated. A part of Emma had hoped that Dan wouldn't ask that question. Her instinctive reaction was that Dan wouldn't want her to do what they were about to do – not without him. Lizzy had cautioned against telling him, saying that it would just cause him to worry unnecessarily.

Emma looked across at her before deciding to come clean. 'We're going to the offices of the *Daily Post*.'

'Oh. Why?' His tone was underscored with concern.

Noting Dan's reaction, Emma continued. 'Adrian Spencer has been following us again. David Sherborn spotted him on Monday, tailing us. He was taking photographs, too.'

'So you're going to do what?' Again, the concern in his voice was palpable.

'We're going to complain to the *Daily Post*.'

There was a pause. 'Do you think that's wise?'

'It's what I want to do,' Emma replied.

Lizzy furrowed her brow, interested in what Dan was saying.

'Just be careful. And tell Lizzy not to get carried away.'

'She'll behave herself.' Emma smiled as her friend looked on, confused. 'I thought you might try and convince me out of it.'

'Well, I can't say I'm overjoyed at the thought of you two going off and doing this on your own. But he's obviously not taking no for an answer, so I think this is the next logical step.'

'We're just going to report what's been going on, dispassionately and calmly. We're not going to cause a scene.'

'I think that's the best strategy.' Dan sounded more relaxed now. 'These big companies, they don't take kindly to people coming in, ranting and raving. But if you go in there professionally, it opens doors and people listen. At least, that's my experience, whenever we've been dealing with suppliers. And also when people have complained to us. I hope they take it seriously.'

'Thanks. I'll let you know how it goes.'

Lizzy grinned, having worked out that Dan hadn't attempted to put them off their mission.

'Promise me one thing, though,' he added.

'Yes?'

'Promise me you won't do anything today about Guy Roberts. I mean, going to the *Daily Post* about Adrian Spencer is one thing, but I don't like the idea of you rushing in and challenging Guy. I get the distinct impression that he could turn nasty if we're not very careful. And I know it might sound sexist, but I strongly feel that, if we do confront him, I should be there.'

Emma smiled, her heart awash with love. 'It's okay. I feel the same way. We won't do anything about him. Not until we've all had time to think about things.'

'Good. And, Em, call me any time. I don't want you to deal with this on your own.'

'I've got Lizzy.'

'You know what I mean. Remember, too, that this person *is* following you. Be careful. Stay with Lizzy. And keep out in the open.'

Emma glanced around the bus. There was no one who looked like the man who had been following them in Windsor. 'We'll be careful, don't worry.'

'But I do worry. A lot.'

The *Daily Post* headquarters was based in Stratford, East London. The train, running on the Docklands Light Railway, glided out of the city, past the towering, shimmering structures of Canary Wharf, and into London's outskirts. Once a derelict industrial wasteland, Stratford had in recent years been transformed by a massive regeneration programme, catalysed by the siting of the London Olympic Stadium in the area.

'So, how are we going to play this?' Lizzy said as they neared the offices, walking along the busy main road that led into Stratford town centre. 'What if they call Adrian Spencer downstairs? He'll probably be angry, don't you think?'

'Do you think he might be there?' Emma replied, taken aback, as a lorry rumbled past. 'I hadn't thought that far ahead,' she admitted. 'Maybe we should have just called the office to report it.'

Lizzy shook her head. 'Nah, it'll be okay. It's better to get there in person. At least we can make sure our complaint gets heard.'

'I suppose.' Suddenly this seemed like a bad idea, but it felt too late to pull out now.

They reached the building: an ugly, concrete tower block straight from the low point in 1970s architectural design. The structure, right on the main road, had taken a beating from the elements and choking traffic pollution: the windows were smeared with grime, and the words *Daily Post* on the sign at the front entrance were partly concealed by dirt.

They entered through the revolving door and waited for the receptionist to complete a telephone conversation. The reception area was all metal, giving them the impression of being inside a tin can.

'Can I help you?' the receptionist said finally, looking up at them from over her glasses.

'We're here to make a complaint,' Emma began, somewhat hesitantly. She wasn't used to complaining. 'It's about one of your reporters – he's been bothering me and my friends for the past few weeks, and we've just found out he's also been taking photographs of us.'

'Okay.' The woman didn't look surprised. She picked up the telephone again. 'Just one moment, please. I'll see if Dominic is here.'

'Dominic?'

'Our public relations manager. Oh, hello, Dominic? It's Elaine here on Reception. I was wondering if you're free now. We've got two ladies down here who would like to make a complaint against one of our reporters . . . No, I didn't ask that . . . Okay, great, thanks.' She replaced the handset and smiled. 'If you could just wait over there, Dominic will be with you shortly.' She gestured to a row of seats in the corner.

'Public relations manager,' Lizzy whispered. 'He's obviously always on standby,' she added, as they sat down in the faux leather armchairs.

Emma was glad that they hadn't yet said who they were complaining about – at least that way Adrian wouldn't be tipped off. She really didn't want to come face to face with him at this point.

A couple of minutes later a man appeared. He was in his early thirties, smartly dressed in a dark suit and an open-collared, pastel blue shirt. He held out a hand and shook theirs in turn. Emma noted his startlingly blue eyes.

'Hi, I'm Dominic Carter, public relations manager for the *Daily Post*. I hear you've got a complaint?'

Emma nodded. 'It's about—'

He held up a hand. 'If you don't mind, we'll continue behind closed doors. It's best to maintain some privacy with these things, I find.'

'Of course.'

They followed him into a nearby office and took a seat.

'Would you like a drink?'

'I'm okay,' Emma replied, not wanting to prolong the meeting any more than they had to.

'I wouldn't mind a water.' Lizzy smiled.

'Of course,' he said. 'We've got a machine down the hallway. You're sure you don't want anything?' he asked Emma.

'I'm fine,' she reiterated.

He turned back to Lizzy. 'Is a plastic cup okay?'

'Perfect.' Lizzy smiled again.

'You fancy him, don't you?' Emma said, after he had left the office.

'Maybe,' Lizzy replied, with a grin.

Emma rolled her eyes as she smiled at her friend. 'I could tell by the way you were looking at him.'

'So,' Dominic said, re-entering the room, not seeming to notice that he had just interrupted something. He handed Lizzy a brimming cup and clapped his hands together. 'How can I help you?'

Emma glanced at Lizzy for support, then back at Dominic. Suddenly, this all seemed very serious, and part of her now regretted taking this step. Even though Adrian Spencer had been very troublesome, and had refused to take no for an answer, she didn't want him to lose his job over this. And by doing what they were doing, it was possible that he could be fired – especially with all the recent controversy about standards in journalism, and the need to demonstrate to the public that the press worked to an ethical code. Once they had made their complaint and left the building, who knew what might happen to him? But still, something did need to be done; hopefully, Adrian's superiors would simply warn him about his behaviour and that would be the end of it. 'One of your journalists has been bothering us,' she said.

'Pestering us,' Lizzy emphasised. 'For *weeks*. Refusing to leave us alone when we said we didn't want to talk to him.' She looked at Emma by way of an apology for her impromptu interjection.

'Okay,' Dominic said, his brow furrowed. 'Maybe I should start by taking your names.'

Emma nodded. 'I'm Emma Holden, and—'

'Lizzy,' Lizzy interrupted, trying on a flirtatious smile. 'Lizzy Thomas.'

Dominic looked up from his notepad, interested, but not, it appeared, in the attention from Lizzy. It was then that she noticed he was wearing a wedding ring. *Darn it!* 'Emma Holden, as in the kidnapping case?'

Emma nodded.

'I see. So, tell me more about what's been happening.'

'Well, as Lizzy said, the reporter, he started approaching us, at home and in the street, trying to get quotes for a feature he's writing on what happened to us. We've told him we aren't interested, but he won't leave us alone. And I've just found out that he's been following me, taking photographs.'

Dominic frowned. 'We've got very strict standards here at the *Daily Post*. Obviously our journalists have to work hard to get their stories, but there is a line, and from what you've just told me, on this occasion, we've crossed it. So, first of all, I'd like to apologise on behalf of the newspaper for what has happened. And, secondly, I want to promise you that we'll speak to the journalist in question, and ensure that this doesn't happen again.'

'Thank you,' Emma said. 'We don't want him to get into trouble. We just want him to leave us alone. We've all been through so much, and we really don't want to be part of another newspaper story. We want privacy, and time to get over it all.'

'It's okay. I understand. He'll just get an informal warning and, like I said, it won't happen again.'

'Thanks.'

'So, if you can just give me his name—?'

Emma looked across at Lizzy again, then back at Dominic. Once she said the name, there was no going back. 'His name is Adrian Spencer.'

'Adrian Spencer,' he said, his pen hovering above the pad. He looked off towards his left, trawling his mind. 'Not familiar with him.' He thought some more. 'Nope, doesn't ring any bells. That's a good thing. It means he can't have been in any trouble before now.' He scribbled down the name. 'Just a second.' He stood up and dialled an extension number on a phone that hung on the wall. 'Veronica? Adrian Spencer – can you just check which team he's based in? He's leading on a feature about the Emma Holden case . . . Thanks.' He waited for a few moments, smiling politely as Emma and Lizzy looked on. His smile disappeared. 'Are you sure? You're absolutely definite about that? Couldn't be a mistake? Okay, thanks, that's brilliant. Much appreciated.'

He sat back down. 'I'm really sorry, but the guy who's been bothering you doesn't work for this newspaper.'

Emma was taken aback. 'Sorry?'

'We don't have anyone called Adrian Spencer working here.'

'But he's writing the article,' Lizzy said. 'The feature article for your paper.'

'There is no feature article being written about you – my PA just checked. I'm sorry, but it looks like he's working for someone else.'

23

Will Holden couldn't concentrate at all. He sat back in his chair and stared out of the window. His work as a human resources officer in the local council wasn't the most stimulating job in the world. It had its moments – mostly when things went wrong – but it wasn't what he'd call an exciting environment. That hadn't bothered him before, but now he felt like he wanted something more, something that was a challenge.

It's amazing how one person can come into your life and shake things up so much, transforming your outlook and worldview in a heartbeat.

He glanced at his watch. It would be lunchtime at her school, but he resisted calling Amy. He didn't want to bother her at work – no doubt she would be busy preparing for the afternoon's lessons, or in discussions with fellow teachers.

Will caught the eye of John, a colleague, who clocked him daydreaming, so he turned his attention back to his computer screen and began typing out the job advert he had been trying to put together for the past hour.

Then his phone rang. His heart leapt when he saw the caller ID. It was Amy.

'Hey,' she said, bright and breezy as always. 'I thought I'd give you a quick call while I was free.'

'Amy, it's great to hear from you.' John was looking openly interested now, so Will moved away from his desk and out into the stairwell. 'I was just thinking about you.'

'Good to hear it.'

Will tapped his fingers absent-mindedly against the bannister. 'So, has your day been good?'

'Ah, not bad, you know. Some of the kids were a bit naughty, but that's nothing unusual. How about you?'

'Pretty dull, to be honest. I'm supposed to be drafting a job pack, but I can't concentrate. I keep thinking about the other day, you know, at the zoo and the London Eye. I'm still buzzing from it, and I guess everything else seems boring.'

'I know what you need.'

'What's that?'

'Something to look forward to. Which is why I've planned something *amazing* for tomorrow, if you can make it.'

'Really?'

'You know I mentioned a parachute jump—?'

His nervousness was instant. 'Well . . . yeah.'

'I forgot to mention that I'm a qualified instructor.'

'O-kaaay.'

'Which means that I'm qualified to do tandem skydives.'

Bloody hell! 'I'm not sure I like where this is going.'

'And I'd like you to accompany me on a skydive, tomorrow afternoon.'

Will could hear the smile in her voice, while he just felt sick. He reached for the bannister to steady himself. The thought of going up in a small plane was horrifying enough, but to then jump out of it – well, that was truly terrifying.

When he replied, he tried not to sound too evasive. 'But don't you have to train for weeks before doing something like that?'

'Not with a tandem jump. You only have to do about fifteen minutes of preparation.'

'Right.'

Fifteen minutes' preparation!

'It's all very safe,' Amy reassured. 'You'd be strapped onto me, and I'd be the one doing everything. I'd pull the cord, and make sure we land safely. You'd just be there to enjoy the ride.'

'Enjoy the ride,' he repeated. 'But doesn't it take time to organise this sort of thing? We'd have to book in somewhere.'

'My friend runs the club where I jump,' she explained. 'It's a small airfield in Essex, just outside the M25. I've already checked with him, and we're all good to go, two o'clock tomorrow. Sorry it's such late notice, but they've managed to squeeze us in – weekends are booked up for weeks in advance. I know you said it's usually easy for you to get time off, so I went for it. He's even given me a big discount. So, are you ready for your biggest challenge yet, Mr Holden?'

Everything about the jump scared him. But he was in love, and to his own great surprise, that proved much stronger than any fear. 'Yes, I'm ready.'

'I don't really know what this all means,' Emma said, as they retraced their steps back towards the Stratford DLR station.

'Adrian Spencer was lying to us, for a start,' Lizzy replied. 'God knows why.'

Emma stopped. Suddenly she wanted to take control. For too long, these external forces, these people, had been controlling their lives, playing with them as if they were marionettes. But it had to stop. '*He* knows. Let's call him.'

Even Lizzy looked shocked by this. 'Call Adrian Spencer. Are you sure?'

'Yes, let's do it,' Emma said, the desperation to find out the truth strengthening her determination. 'We can meet him somewhere public, and then ask him face to face what the hell he's doing.'

She pulled out her phone and dialled the number she had stored for Adrian Spencer, following his initial call some weeks ago. Only then did the nerves kick in, but she did her best not to reveal them.

'Hi, is that Adrian? It's Emma Holden here. I've decided that I am prepared to talk. I'm free now, if that's convenient . . . Great, so we could meet somewhere in the centre. How about the coffee shop in Foyles bookshop on Charing Cross Road, in an hour? That's great, see you then.' She ended the call.

'I've done it,' Emma said as she dropped her phone in her pocket, as much to herself as Lizzy.

'Are you really sure about this?' Lizzy said. 'I mean, I know I'm normally the one to jump at the chance of challenging this kind of thing, but it could be risky. Not to mention the fact that there is this other person still out there, following you. I mean, Dan was right in what he said, about needing to be careful. I don't think he'd want us to be challenging Adrian Spencer on our own.' She looked at Emma. 'After all, we don't really know what he's like, as a person, do we? And we certainly don't know how he'll react when we tell him he's a liar.'

'You're right,' said Emma. 'I'll call Dan. He needs to be there, too.'

'Stephen, isn't it?' The curly-haired, middle-aged woman smiled as she stood at the door to her home in Camden.

He nodded, but didn't say anything, and didn't return the smile.

Seemingly unfazed by his silence and stony expression, she maintained the smile and held out a hand, which he shook. 'Please, do come in.' She stood back to let him pass. 'I've got a little room out at the back, which I use for consultations,' she explained, as he followed her through a living room and kitchen, and out of a side door.

They entered a small room, which had two chairs facing each other and a small, round coffee table. The bookshelves on the walls held various counselling and psychotherapy textbooks. 'It's nice and private,' she added. 'Please, take a seat and make yourself comfortable.'

He took off his jacket. It would be easier to show her what he had done.

He had found Doreen Smithson on the internet. A mental health nurse, she had trained in psychotherapy and was offering sessions at a reasonable rate for those suffering from a range of mental health issues, including anxiety. Here he could talk about his past and present feelings, his experiences, and his desires. It was the perfect opportunity to improve himself, to once again

169

show that he was prepared to go that extra mile in pursuit of that which he desired so strongly.

She smiled again, her hands on her knees. 'So, Stephen, how can I help?'

'I'm in love with a girl,' he began, unblinking, as he looked straight into her eyes. 'But she's with someone else.'

'Okay,' she replied. 'And that makes you feel—?'

He thought for a few seconds. 'Sad,' he said, finally. 'And angry. *Very* angry.'

She nodded, but didn't reveal any emotional reaction. 'Angry because you can't be with this girl?'

'Yes.'

'And how has this anger manifested itself, Stephen?'

He decided not to hold back. 'Bad thoughts. About death. About dying.'

Now there seemed to be a reaction, a tiny flicker. 'Right. When you say thoughts about death, do you mean suicide?'

'No.'

There was definitely a reaction now. *Fear?* Possibly.

'Then how do you mean?'

'I just want him to disappear,' he stated.

'Who? The man she is with?'

'Yes.'

'You've had thoughts about him?'

'Yes. About killing him.'

She nodded, smooth-faced. She was pretty professional, he had to give her that. 'But you've not acted on those thoughts, have you?'

'No.'

That seemed to reassure her. 'A lot of people fantasise, Stephen. Sometimes we fantasise about doing bad things. But that is very different to actually carrying out those fantasies.'

'I understand.'

'Have you ever spoken to anyone else about these thoughts and feelings? Your doctor? Your family?'

'No.'

'The important thing is that you've taken the first step, Stephen – you contacted me and booked an appointment. And here you are now, talking about things for the first time. Don't underestimate how significant that first step asking for help is.' She nodded at him, reassuringly. 'What made you take that first step, if you don't mind me asking?'

He shrugged. 'I don't know.'

'Well, what matters is that you've taken it, for whatever reason. Can you tell me about this girl?'

'I can show you her,' he replied.

She sat forward. *Feigning interest*, he thought.

'Oh, you have a photo?'

'No, not a photograph.'

He pulled his jumper over his head, and undid the top buttons of his shirt, revealing a tattoo on his left shoulder.

'Oh,' she said. 'That's her, is it?'

'Yes,' he replied. 'Emma. I've just had it done. The tattooist copied it from a photograph that I had of her. Beautiful, isn't she?'

'Yes, she is. Why did you have the tattoo done, Stephen?'

He smiled. This time he would tell the truth. 'To demonstrate my total commitment.'

24

Emma and Lizzy neared the bookshop, which was situated along Charing Cross Road, a little way down from the salsa bar where, just over four weeks ago, Emma had rescued a drunken and emotionally fraught Will from the middle of the road.

Emma shook her head as she looked out into the road at the spot where it happened, remembering the incident. Those had been terrible times, to which she hoped she would never have to return again.

'Are you okay, Em?' Lizzy asked.

'Yeah, I'm just thinking back to how bad Will was, with that awful secret of being involved in Stephen Myers' death all bottled up inside. That night at the salsa club, he was right on the edge. I didn't know it at the time, but it was serious.'

'I know.'

'It's so good to see him happy now.' Emma and Lizzy had bumped into Will and his new girlfriend during a shopping trip, the week before. He hadn't stopped talking about her since.

'Definitely.'

Will had called her five minutes before, and she had updated him on what had happened during the day, including the revelations of David Sherborn about the connection between Guy Roberts and the man who was following them, as well as the news that Adrian Spencer was not in fact working for the *Daily Post*. Will had been concerned about their plans, but glad to hear that Dan was on his way to meet them, in time for their meeting with Adrian.

Except that as Emma and Lizzy reached the shop, just ten minutes before Adrian Spencer was due to arrive, Dan was out of contact. Emma had tried to call him several times without success: each time the call had gone straight through to the messaging service.

They stopped outside the entrance. Dan wasn't there. 'I was hoping Dan might have been waiting for us here,' Emma said, disappointment and worry evident in her voice.

'Maybe he's upstairs already, in the café?'

'Maybe. I guess as our meeting place was definite, then he'd just head straight for the coffee shop.'

They hurried up the stairs and across the upper level to the coffee area.

He wasn't there either.

'I'll try him again.' Emma dialled Dan's number, but once again it cut straight through to the answer service. 'Nothing. It's either his battery's run out, or maybe he's been delayed en route. If he's stuck on the tube, then that would explain why it isn't ringing through.'

'You're probably right.' Lizzy looked at her watch. 'Adrian Spencer will be here in a few minutes.'

'I know.' Emma really didn't want him to arrive before Dan, but if they had to do it alone, they would.

They ordered two coffees and took a seat at a table for four. Emma looked around. This had been a good choice of venue, as it was very public. The small coffee-shop area was integrated with the bookshop, in an open-plan style that encouraged users to browse books while they sipped. It was one of the innovative features of the newly redesigned bookshop that had enabled it to succeed where other, bigger bookstores had failed in recent years. It also offered something that online stores couldn't: atmosphere. The bookshop was a favourite for them all and, as such, it felt like home territory for Emma. But still, she didn't relish tackling Adrian Spencer without Dan's support.

She looked over towards the stairs and her stomach turned. 'He's here.'

'Dan?'

'No.'

Lizzy looked round and saw Adrian Spencer approaching. He was a few minutes early.

He sauntered over to them and took the seat opposite, smiling. 'Hello there. I didn't expect to see you too, Lizzy.'

'Change of heart,' Lizzy said, unsmiling.

'Great, great,' he said, delving into his bag and pulling out his notebook and a digital recorder, which he placed on the table. 'I'm glad you've seen sense.'

Lizzy had to bite her tongue.

'So,' he said, 'shall we get started?'

'Is it okay if I ask a question first?' Emma glanced over his shoulder in the hope that Dan might appear, but there was still no sign of him.

'Of course, fire away.'

Emma had been rehearsing this conversation in her mind for the past hour, but now the pre-planned lines were hazy. 'You said you're doing a feature article for the *Daily Post*.'

Adrian looked calm and confident. 'Yes, that's right. Now that you're cooperating, it should be ready to go next week.'

Emma was feeling nervous – they would have to play this carefully. She tried her best to look relaxed, wondering if her face gave away her true state. 'Who asked you to do it?'

He looked confused – or was it defensive? 'Well, my boss, of course. The editor.'

'Who is—?'

He did his best not to look rattled, but Emma could tell that he didn't have a name to hand. 'If you want to talk to my seniors, then I'd be happy to put you in touch with them.'

'It's okay,' Emma replied. 'That won't be necessary. How long have you worked at the newspaper?'

Now she could hear the nerves in her voice. It was surely a dead giveaway.

But Adrian Spencer didn't seem to notice. 'Well . . . six, seven years.'

'Do you enjoy it?'

'Yes, I do.'

'Why are you lying to us?' Lizzy said.

He feigned shock. 'What?'

Lizzy pressed home her point. 'You don't work for the *Post*, do you?'

His eyes darted around the room.

Emma gathered some more courage. 'We know you don't work for the newspaper. We went there today. They've never heard of you.'

Now he smiled and held up his hands in surrender. 'Bravo. You got me.'

Emma continued the interrogation. 'Who are you?'

'Adrian Spencer,' he replied.

'You know what I mean. You were following me, taking photographs. Why?'

'I'd better be going,' he said, moving to get up. 'Things to do, people to see.'

But as he went to rise, he was pressed back down into his chair by someone he hadn't noticed arriving just seconds earlier: Dan.

'An ambush.' Adrian twisted to look up at Dan, who kept a hand on his shoulder in a way that an onlooker might interpret as simply a friendly gesture.

Dan smiled. 'You can call it whatever you like.'

Adrian turned back to Emma and Lizzy. 'Okay. I'll tell you. I don't want there to be any animosity between us.' He looked at them. 'I'm a researcher, working for Firework Films.'

Emma shook her head. 'I should have known.' Firework Films – the production company that had wanted to make the docudrama about them.

Well, if this is the way they go about conducting their research, I'm doubly glad I dismissed their offer.

'Look,' he said, 'I know I've probably gone about this the wrong way – I should have been upfront with you. To be honest,

I don't know why I used that cover story. It was stupid, I understand that.'

Emma didn't want to hear it. 'You wanted to cover your bases, in case I said no to Diana Saunders about collaborating on the programme. You wanted to get quotes from us, and that way you could still go ahead with the production, without our direct input. You figured that we would be more likely to provide a few quotes for a newspaper article. And if I'd said yes to Diana, then no doubt someone else from Firework Films would have been liaising with us, and we'd never have connected you and your shady practices with them.'

Adrian looked back at her, genuinely bemused. 'I don't know why you won't just cooperate,' he said. 'I mean, this is a *great* opportunity for you all. And particularly you, Emma.'

'A great opportunity for Firework Films to exploit the situation,' Lizzy said.

'Yes,' Emma agreed. 'They're exploiting a very personal situation.'

Adrian shrugged. '*Someone* will make commercial gain from what happened. It's just too good a story. I mean, it has everything – drama, mystery, twists and turns. And, most importantly, a happy ending. If it isn't Firework Films, it will be someone else, believe me. There's nothing you can do about it, so why not just go with the flow?'

'Because we don't want to,' Dan said, his hand still on Adrian's shoulder.

'Firework aren't evil, you know. They just want to make the most entertaining – and accurate – programme that they can make.'

Lizzy laughed. 'I've seen some of their programmes. They're exploitative, and cheap, and I'm sure not at all accurate.'

'But I bet you just *had* to watch them, didn't you?' Adrian mocked.

'They deceived us,' Lizzy shot back.

Adrian remained unrepentant. 'The offer Diana made to you, Emma – to be involved with the docudrama – was an open one.'

'How did you persuade Diana to become involved?' Emma asked. 'How did you persuade her to approach me?'

'She didn't need persuading. As I said, it's a great story. She knows, more than most, when something will be big and has great commercial value. She's one of the best in the business at spotting the next big thing. People like Diana don't waste their time on things that aren't going to be money-spinners.' He paused and looked at her confidently. 'So are you sure you won't reconsider?'

Emma couldn't quite believe the persistence and cheek of him. Here he was, being presented with the evidence that he was a liar, and he remained as brazen as ever. Suddenly she was furious. 'There's absolutely no chance of that. We would *never* work with a company that has set out to deceive us. So you won't be getting *any*thing from any of us.'

Adrian smiled. 'Oh, really? Are you sure about that?'

'Of course,' Emma said.

'You might be surprised.'

Emma suddenly had an awful feeling about where this was going. 'What do you mean?'

He smiled again. 'You know, I wish you were as helpful as your father.'

'What?' An icy finger slid down Emma's spine.

'It's just that if you were all as open as he was, it would make the programme so much better, so much more *powerful*, to really know what was going on in your heads.'

Emma felt sick. He had to be lying. She shook her head. 'He didn't talk to you. He wouldn't have done that.' But then she remembered the note her father had left. He had mentioned being sorry.

Maybe this is what he was sorry about.

'Oh, he did, Emma – he was very open and honest, extremely insightful, and spent quite a deal of time talking to me. But don't worry, he was generously reimbursed for his time. *Generously reimbursed.*'

He went to stand, and Emma nodded at Dan to let him go. She was reeling at the revelation.

But Adrian Spencer hadn't quite finished. 'Next time you see him, pass on my thanks on behalf of Firework Films.'

25

As soon as they got back to the flat they called the production company, Firework Films. During the walk home, Emma, Dan and Lizzy had decided that it was possibly the only chance they had of dealing with the situation. Adrian had been unrepentant, and had walked off shortly after his revelation that Edward had spoken to him, offering no guarantees that he would leave them alone. Maybe by talking to the company itself, they would have more success.

The telephone number for the company was available freely on their website, and Emma keyed it into her mobile. Dan had offered to talk to them, but Emma thought that it would be more powerful coming from her.

A woman answered. 'Firework Films. How can I help you?'

'Hello,' Emma said. She was sitting at the kitchen table, with Dan and Lizzy looking on. 'My name's Emma Holden, and I would like to talk to someone about one of the company's projects.'

'Okay,' the woman replied. 'Is this about a programme that you've seen?'

'No, it's a programme that's currently being made.'

'Right. And are you—?'

'I'm supposed to be featuring in the programme,' Emma finished. 'Well, me and my friends are the subjects of the docudrama.'

'Okay. And you said your name is—?'

'Emma. Emma Holden.'

'Emma, great. One moment please, I'm just putting you through to our production team.'

Emma prayed that Adrian Spencer wasn't about to appear on the other end of the line. That would be uncomfortable beyond belief. 'They've put me through to the production department,' she said, covering the mouthpiece with her hand. The other two nodded, as a new voice spoke.

'Hello, production team. Nikki speaking.' The voice was bright and friendly, but Emma wondered how much this might change before the end of the conversation.

'Hi. My name's Emma Holden. I'm calling about—'

'Emma! Hello! So great to hear from you!' Now the girl just seemed false, like so many of the entertainment types that Emma had met in her career so far. There were many genuine people in the industry, without doubt; Emma had been fortunate enough to work with many such people. But there was also a significant minority who were prepared to say one thing to a person's face, and quite another behind their back – whatever it took to advance their career and achieve their goals. 'What can I do for you? I guess you're calling about the docudrama?'

'Yes,' Emma said. 'I am.'

'Great! How can I help?' Her reaction was surprisingly positive. There was no hint of concern in her voice.

Has she really not heard from Adrian Spencer about what just happened?

'I want to make a request,' Emma said.

'Sure.'

'I want to ask that your company stays away from me, my friends and family.'

'Okay.' Now Nikki didn't sound so positive. 'Is there something . . . have we done something to upset you?

'One of your researchers, Adrian Spencer, has been pestering us for the past few weeks. He's been following us, taking photographs, phoning us. We've asked him to stop, but he doesn't seem to get the message.'

'I'm sorry to hear that.'

'We just want to be left alone,' Emma said. 'Of course, we'd prefer it if there was no programme at all, but at the least, we don't wish to be any part of it.'

'Understood. We won't bother you again. I'm really sorry that you've had this experience. It's really not the way we like to go about doing things, I assure you.'

Emma smiled at the other two, to let them know that it seemed to be going well. 'As long as it stops now, then that's the end of it as far as we're concerned. We want to get on with our lives, without being hassled.'

'Of course. And again, I'm very sorry. It would, of course, have been great to have had your input with the production – we obviously want to be as accurate as possible with how we portray events, and your input would have helped to ensure this. But we do understand if you feel that you don't want to take part.'

Emma took her reasonable words with a large pinch of salt.

Surely they already know that we don't want to participate? Unless, of course, Adrian Spencer has never reported this back . . .

'So will you continue with the production, regardless?' Emma asked.

'Almost certainly, yes,' Nikki said. 'We're some way into the production process, and we did factor in this scenario at the outset. It's certainly unfortunate from our point of view, but it's not fatal.'

Emma was disappointed. 'I wondered if you might say that.' She hadn't believed with any certainty that, without their support, the docudrama would be cancelled, but it had been a hope. Now, with that wish seemingly dashed, they would all have to get used to the fact that perhaps, sometime in the future, the programme would air. It wouldn't be pleasant, but Emma hoped that everyone would be in a much better place by then, and able to withstand the bad memories and unwanted attention.

'We will strive to be as compassionate as possible in the way we portray what happened to you all,' Nikki continued, smoothly.

'Thank you, that would be much appreciated.' Having seen some of their other productions, Emma found it hard to believe.

'I still can't believe he would have done it. I just feel so angry.'

Emma, Dan and Lizzy were still in the flat. It was late afternoon, and they were back in the kitchen, sitting around the table. Now that Emma had dealt with Firework Films, she was reeling again from what Adrian Spencer had told them. The thought that her dad had spoken to that man, for money, really hurt.

'It does explain the note that he left Miranda,' Lizzy said. 'About being sorry.'

'It sounds like he regrets doing it,' Dan added. 'Try not to be too hard on him.'

'Do you think that's why he ran away?' mused Emma. This was all now starting to make sense. 'Because he realised what he'd done was wrong, and just couldn't face us?'

Dan shrugged. 'Maybe. Look, I'm not making excuses for him – well, maybe I am – but Adrian Spencer *was* extremely persistent, *and* he was offering money to someone who's been really worried about his income. You know how he's been stressing about losing his clients, and Miranda mentioned that he'd been worried about not being able to support her and the baby, just before he left. I know he's brought some of this on himself, but the guy is obviously really suffering.'

'Your dad's been under a lot of pressure,' Lizzy acknowledged. 'He might have just got tempted, and then really regretted it.'

Emma could see how it might have happened.

Just a few minutes of your time …

I can recompense you …

This way we can make sure we get the story straight …

'You're probably right,' she said, 'but running away isn't going to solve anything. It just makes things worse. He's abandoned Miranda and caused even more hurt. Can't he see that?'

'Maybe now that he's run,' suggested Dan, 'he doesn't know how to come back and make things right. He might feel too ashamed about it all. He also might genuinely believe that we don't want to see him again.'

Emma shook her head. 'I just wish he'd get in contact, or turn his phone back on. At least we'd know he's safe.'

'Safe?' Lizzy said. 'You think he might not be?'

'Oh, I'm sure he's fine,' Emma said, 'but we don't know that for certain. If he is in such a state, then we don't know what he might do. People can do really irrational things when they're not thinking straight. When Mum died, he got really low.'

'But not low enough to . . .' Lizzy trailed off.

'I don't think he ever went as far as wanting to end things,' Emma replied. 'But then again, he probably wouldn't have told me if that's what he had been thinking. I've always thought that he might still be vulnerable, despite the strong-man act that he puts on sometimes. I just hope he doesn't do something stupid.' Emma shook her head. 'If only we could talk to him, tell him that this is fixable.'

'We've got to stay positive,' Dan advised. 'I'm sure it won't be long before you hear from him. After all, he's got a wonderful family and a baby on the way. He won't want to lose that.'

'You're right,' Emma replied, hauling herself out of her negativity with an effort.

'Do you think that Adrian Spencer will leave us alone, now that we've complained directly to the company?' Lizzy asked.

'Well,' said Emma grimly, 'with Firework Films still going ahead with the docudrama, there's no guarantee, is there?'

'No, I guess not.'

'Hopefully he will,' Emma added.

'At least if he crawls back into his hole that'll be one thing off our backs,' Lizzy said. 'But the bigger worry is this other person pretending to be Stephen Myers.'

'I still can't believe he followed us to Windsor,' Dan said. 'He must have tailed us from first thing that morning, otherwise how would he have known we were going there? To think that he's probably been stalking us to the flat, and the police aren't interested.'

'I know,' Emma said. 'David Sherborn only started following us from the train station after I texted him to let him know where we were going, but this guy was already there when he arrived. He had to have followed us from here.'

'Creepy,' Lizzy said. 'It's just like last time.'

'Except that this time we're not helpless victims,' Dan said. 'Last time, you didn't know anything about what was happening and who was involved. But this time, because we enlisted David Sherborn's help – because we took the initiative – we at least have some information on this person. We know that he knows Guy Roberts.'

'And we also know that it isn't actually Stephen Myers who is doing this,' Lizzy added.

'Exactly,' Dan said. 'And even though it was pretty crazy to think that it was Stephen Myers, someone wanted us to think that. If we hadn't done what we did, identifying the person who is doing this, then there might still be that element of doubt. Especially given what Peter Myers had said to you, Lizzy, about Stephen being alive.'

'Which he must have said just to scare us,' Lizzy said.

'That's right.'

'So the next step is to go and see Guy Roberts,' Emma said, with finality. 'And find out what he knows about this person. And how they're linked.'

'Do you think he'll tell us?' Lizzy asked. 'I mean, we can't assume he'll cooperate. We know what kind of person he is.'

'I agree it might be difficult. I'm not assuming anything.'

'And we can't trust him either,' Dan replied. 'But we haven't really got any other options, have we?'

'No,' Lizzy said.

'So the question is, when?'

Emma glanced at the clock. 'How about after we eat?'

Lizzy raised an eyebrow. 'Not tomorrow morning? I thought we might want to sleep on it.'

'He's more likely to be in at night, don't you think?' Emma replied.

'And I want to be there, too,' Dan added. 'Work gets in the way again tomorrow.'

'Okay,' Lizzy said. 'At least it gets it over with. So, we eat first and then go and see him. Who votes for a chippy tea?'

'Sounds good to me,' Emma said. 'Although let's eat now, before I lose my appetite thinking about having to see that man again.'

26

'Emma, how *nice* to see you.' Guy Roberts, his white hair still in its trendy, messy style, stood at the front door of his sleek Notting Hill home: the place where, just four weeks before, Emma had walked out on her dream of starring in the movie that he was casting. She hadn't regretted it for a moment. And now, seeing this man acting so friendly, after everything he had done, cemented the belief that she had definitely made the right decision.

That, and the fact that she had also stood on this very doorstep to berate him for employing someone to take photos of her for the tabloids. *I can't believe he'd have done it again. What sort of person* is *he?*

She would rather walk away from the business than be associated with people like Guy Roberts – or Diana Saunders, for that matter.

'Can we come in for a moment?' she asked.

Only then did Guy look at her companions, as if he'd only just noticed them. He played with his silver earring as he considered their presence. 'Certainly. Come on through.'

They followed him past original, framed movie posters, and into the lounge with the piano in the corner. Emma had already told Dan and Lizzy how amazing the house was, resembling an upmarket show home.

'Take a seat,' said Guy, gesturing towards the plush leather chairs. 'Can I get you a drink?'

Emma remained standing. 'We're okay, thanks.'

He looked at Dan, and then Lizzy. 'Are you sure?'

Dan was stony-faced. 'I'm fine, thank you.'

'I'm okay, too,' Lizzy added.

'Right, then.' For a second Guy seemed a little slighted at the rejection of his hospitality. 'So, what can I do for you, Emma? I'm afraid if you've changed your mind about the movie role, we've already found a replacement. You've heard of Jenna Dawson?'

'I've heard of her, yes.'

Jenna Dawson was an up-and-coming soap actress, about the same age as Emma. There were definite parallels in their careers. They had both impressed in soap operas, being then slated for better things. Rumour had it that Jenna had been shortlisted for the part of the assistant in *Doctor Who*. And now it seemed that the big movie break that was to have been Emma's was now hers.

Guy smiled. 'Then you'll know that she's a real talent. I think she's got what it takes to go right to the top.'

'I'm sure she'll be perfect for the part.'

Emma had little doubt that Guy Roberts was still bitter about her pulling out of the movie, even though he had been the one to blame. But she wouldn't rise to the bait. They were here for a single reason – to find out who the stalker was. And as Guy was the only person who could tell them what they needed to know, it wouldn't be sensible to be anything other than polite to him.

'Oh, she will,' he replied. 'She's a true professional.'

Emma continued to hold her tongue, but she could see Lizzy bristling with anger. 'The reason we're here is nothing to do with the movie,' Emma explained. 'We need your help.'

Guy looked amused. 'My help? That's a turn up. Go on.'

'Someone came to see you yesterday.'

He didn't give anything away, remaining expressionless. 'A few people came to see me yesterday.'

Emma sensed he was toying with her, but if she had to spell it out, she would. 'A man, in his mid-twenties, tall, dark-brown hair – he came to see you yesterday afternoon. We'd like to know who he is.'

Guy took a moment to reply. 'Two questions – one, why do you want to know? And two, *how* do you know who has been visiting my home?'

'Someone has been following me,' Emma replied.

Guy's face exploded into a grin and he clapped his hands together with glee. '*Another* stalker! Oh, Emma, you do attract them, don't you?'

She ignored the jibe. 'We know it's the person who came to see you. We know he visited you because a friend of ours was following him.'

She wasn't going to give away David Sherborn's involvement: he didn't need or deserve to be part of this.

'You don't think I'm something to do with this, do you?' he asked, suddenly serious.

Emma wasn't sure whether his expression was just another form of him mocking her.

'We just want to know who the person is,' Dan said forcefully. 'Because from where we're standing, it looks like you're up to your neck in this. Again.' He leant meaningfully on the last word.

Guy shot him a look. 'I've not done anything wrong. Whatever this idiot is up to, it's nothing to do with me.'

There was a silence.

Guy Roberts was starting to look uncharacteristically worried. 'Look, I know I got that David bloke to follow you, but I'd be crazy to do the same thing again, wouldn't I? After all' – he seemed to be regaining some of his usual arrogance – 'I've got bigger fish to fry now, haven't I? Why would I want to rock the boat?'

It did make sense, Emma had to concede.

Lizzy spoke for the first time. 'Then just tell us who he is, at least.'

'As Dan said, we just want to know who he is,' Emma said. 'Please, tell us.'

Guy smiled, obviously enjoying the fact he'd regained the position of power. 'Okay, I'll tell you.'

He hadn't intended to visit the flat that evening, but he had found himself drawn to being near Emma Holden. He travelled over to Marylebone and waited across the road, gazing up at her window. Then, just ten minutes after he arrived, the three of them – Emma, Dan and Lizzy – exited. He followed them from the flat, intrigued as to where they were going that evening. Something, maybe their purposeful pace, told him it wasn't for pleasure. Keeping what he felt was a safe distance, he tailed them to the tube. This was always the riskiest part of the journey, as he had to travel in the same carriage, otherwise he wouldn't know which station they got off at. He sat as far away as he could, partly shielded by one of the partitions.

He didn't watch them too obviously, for fear of being spotted; he wasn't in character, however, so there was no reason for them to suspect anything. To them, he would be just another young Londoner, riding the tube.

When they alighted at Notting Hill Gate, he started getting worried.

Could they know?

But the thought was just preposterous. There was no way they could know. And yet, they were heading straight for his house . . .

Guy built up the tension to unbearable levels, retreating to a minibar in the corner of the room and pouring himself a Scotch. He returned, swilling the liquid around his glass. 'His name,' he said, taking a sip of the Scotch, 'is Scott Goulding.'

Emma breathed an inward sigh of relief that he had at last given them a name. For a second, she had thought that he might be just setting them up for a big disappointment. 'Is he a friend of yours?'

Guy snorted, knocking back the rest of the Scotch in one. 'Hardly. He's a real headache. The man thinks he's acting's next big thing, but I'm afraid he's more than a little delusional. Since auditioning for me for a film role six months ago – and failing miserably – he refuses to take no for an answer. I'm this far,' he said, indicating with his finger and thumb, 'from calling the police and reporting him. He was back yesterday, begging to be given a part in one of my new projects. I told him there was no chance. I'm running a business, not a charity for third-rate actors.'

So he's an actor.

Desperate for every scrap of information that she could get on this character, Emma prayed that Guy would remain cooperative in the face of her questions. 'What do you know about him?'

'Very little, but more than I'd like.'

'Do you have any contact details?'

'I may have.'

'Please . . .' Emma said.

'Okay, okay. I have his address. Just wait here while I get it.'

'I really don't trust him,' Lizzy whispered, once Guy was out of the room.

'Me, neither,' Emma replied.

But already Guy was back. 'Here you go,' he said, handing Emma a piece of paper. The address was a flat in Hackney. There was also a mobile number. 'So what exactly has he been doing, then?'

Emma wondered whether to tell him, and risk further ridicule. 'He's been stalking me, pretending to be Stephen Myers.'

'Method acting.' Guy nodded, impressed. 'Maybe I misjudged his abilities.'

'Is there anything else you can tell us about Scott?' Emma said.

'I'm afraid not,' he said, looking at his watch, pointedly. 'I'm going to be late for a meeting. Sorry, people, time for me to go.'

27

They called the police as soon as they got back to the flat. Armed with a name and an address, plus the evidence from David Sherborn, they believed that action could now be taken. Two hours later, two uniformed officers arrived to take a statement.

'I'm Police Constable Karen Loughlin,' the older of the officers said, an attractive blonde with a short bob, in her late thirties. As Emma shook her hand, she added, 'And this is my colleague, PC Amy Whittle.' The younger officer smiled, almost shyly. She was obviously a relatively new recruit, of graduate age.

Emma led them into the living room, where Dan and Lizzy stood up to greet them.

They quickly got down to business, with PC Loughlin leading the questioning.

'So, you asked a *photographer* to follow you?' she said, after Emma had outlined the background to the story of how they had garnered the name Scott Goulding.

'Yes, we did,' Emma replied, aware that it did sound a little strange out of context. She felt the need to add more justification for their decision. 'We thought he might be able to identify if anyone was really following us. We knew him, you see. We knew he would be good at it.'

'Okay,' the officer said. 'What makes you sure that this man' – she looked down at her notebook – 'Scott Goulding, is the same person you think was following you in Cornwall?'

'Because, well, we're just sure,' Emma replied, exchanging glances with Dan and Lizzy. 'He matches the description given by the girl in the florist's shop, and he does bear a resemblance to Stephen Myers.'

Again PC Loughlin looked down at her notebook. 'But that's not really enough to go on. If you had a photograph of the person in Cornwall who you think might have been following you, then that would be a different matter. But the fact is, you didn't actually see this person up close, first-hand, did you? You're relying on the recollection of someone else – the girl in the shop. At the moment, it's all very circumstantial.' She smiled at them, tiredly. 'You really don't have any doubts that Scott Goulding is the person in Cornwall?'

Emma felt that she was the one under suspicion, being tested. It wasn't a pleasant feeling. 'No, we didn't see them close up, but I'm sure it's the same person.'

PC Loughlin still looked unconvinced, but didn't challenge her further. 'Do you have any idea what the motive might be for this?'

'No,' Emma said. 'None whatsoever.'

'And you're sure that you haven't come across him during your acting career? Maybe someone who may hold a grudge, for whatever reason. It seems a funny coincidence that he's an actor, too.'

Emma paused. 'I've got to admit, I hadn't thought of it like that. But no, as far as I can remember, I've never met him before. And I've got a good memory for names and faces.'

'Well, thank you for answering our questions,' PC Loughlin said, seemingly satisfied with what she had heard. 'You're right to have reported this. And it's important that you remain vigilant. We would still recommend that you continue to follow the advice you were given at the beginning of the week – report anything suspicious, don't take any unnecessary risks when it comes to your personal safety, that sort of thing. Specifically, we would advise you not to go out alone at night, and to avoid isolated locations. If something does happen that you are concerned about, then phone us straight away. Again, on the issue of personal safety, I would strongly advise you not to try and take the law into your own hands. Let us get on with our job. We don't want any of you risking your wellbeing.'

She and her colleague made to stand.

'What are you going to do?' Lizzy asked. 'You will speak to him, won't you?'

'If we need to speak to him, we've got his name and number,' she replied.

Lizzy's frustration was evident. 'So that's a no?'

Emma shook her head. 'But *why* not talk to him?'

'Because nothing overly sinister has occurred since that episode at the theatre, which may not have been connected to this at all. So that's why our message is one of vigilance. That doesn't mean we're dismissing your concerns, or being complacent with your safety and well-being. Be on your guard. Report anything suspicious. If you do see this man following you, then report it to us straight away.'

'Do you fancy watching a film?' Dan asked, as they all settled down in the living room.

'Something light,' Lizzy said, stretching back on the sofa. 'A romcom maybe. I need to be taken away from what's going on.'

They decided to go for a comedy, the Alan Partridge movie, but Emma couldn't concentrate. She was still coming to terms with the fact that the police weren't prepared to speak to Scott Goulding. Halfway through the film she got up. 'I'm going to call Miranda,' she said, moving into the kitchen.

She thought explaining their theory about Edward's disappearance might help to reassure Miranda that it wasn't anything to do with her or the baby, but it backfired. Instead of taking any comfort from that, Miranda was troubled by the idea that Edward had betrayed Emma by speaking to Firework Films. By the end of the call, Emma found herself wishing she hadn't said anything.

She then called Will, to update him on what had happened with Adrian Spencer. He was out with Amy, having a meal, but he answered anyway.

Amid all this renewed torment, Will's blossoming relationship with Amy was the one bright spot. It was so good to hear him happy.

'You're doing what?' exclaimed Emma. 'A parachute jump!' She couldn't believe that her brother – the person who, for as long as she could remember, got vertigo at the top of a flight of stairs – would be jumping out of an aeroplane tomorrow. He didn't even sound nervous.

Emma returned to Dan and Lizzy. 'You won't believe what Will is doing tomorrow. A tandem parachute jump!'

'Wow,' Dan said, 'I didn't see that one coming. Where's he doing it?'

'At the airfield of a friend of Amy's, apparently. Just north of the M25.'

'It must be love,' Lizzy said.

'Or insanity,' Dan joked.

For a moment it broke the tension. But they all knew that the serious situation needed talking about.

Emma found herself standing at the window, looking down at the street from behind the curtain. There was no one loitering outside. 'I can't believe this is happening again.'

Dan came over and put an arm around her. 'It's going to be okay, Em, I promise.'

'I hope you're right.'

He pulled her closer. 'It will be. I know it doesn't feel like there's an end to this, but we'll come out the other side.'

Emma sighed. 'For over a month now, ever since Will's phone call on the hen night, it's felt like we're trapped in this nightmare – as if we're in a dark tunnel, walking, sometimes running. Then there's a flicker of light ahead, and you think there's a way out, but the more you move towards it, the further away it seems to get. I thought I was handling this, but now I'm not so sure.'

'Oh, Em, it'll be okay.' Lizzy was standing on her other side now. The three of them were looking down at the street, as the film on the TV behind them continued without an audience.

'So, what do we do?' asked Emma. 'Watch and wait? Or find out what Scott Goulding is playing at?'

That was the question they had all been avoiding since the police left. Should they do nothing, or something?

'I don't know,' Lizzy replied. 'I just don't know. It could be dangerous, just turning up and challenging him.'

'I agree,' Dan said.

Lizzy stepped away from the window and flicked the lights on and the TV off. 'Then we just sit back?'

Dan shook his head. 'No.'

Emma was surprised. 'What are you thinking?'

'We have his telephone number. Why don't we call him, and let him know that he's been found out? Tell him to leave you alone, and let that be the end of it.'

Emma wasn't so sure. 'You think he'll listen to us?'

Dan shrugged. 'Maybe if we pretend to be the police.'

'I like it!' Lizzy replied. 'Just warn him off. It might work.'

'It's still risky.' Emma directed the comment at Dan. 'It might backfire.'

'In what way?'

'I don't know.'

'The alternative,' Dan said, 'is to let him carry on thinking that he's getting away with it, which surely is more likely to mean that he'll carry on doing it. And then what – we wait until something worse happens before the police take action?'

'I guess if he does back off and disappear, we'll never find out why he was doing this,' Lizzy said.

'Probably not,' Dan replied, 'but I think our priority should be putting a stop to this.'

'Okay,' Emma said. 'Let's do it.'

'I don't mind doing the talking,' Dan offered. 'Shall we do this now?'

Emma nodded. 'Why not – get it over with.'

'And then it might all be over,' Lizzy said.

They went into the kitchen and planned what Dan was going to say – he would keep it professional and to the point. They would also ensure that their number was hidden, by keying in 141 before dialling.

A few minutes later, at eleven o'clock, Dan dialled the number that Guy Roberts had given them. He looked at Emma and Lizzy. 'It's ringing.'

Emma felt heartsick as she watched Dan, as the phone rang. Just as she began to relax, thinking that Scott Goulding wasn't going to answer, Dan began talking through the script that they had planned.

'Hello, is that Mr Scott Goulding?' He'd moderated his voice, lowering the tone slightly, just in case the guy knew what he normally sounded like. He nodded at Emma and Lizzy, indicating that they had the right man. 'This is Detective Inspector Mark Gasnier from the Metropolitan Police.' They'd decided to use his name for authenticity. 'We have reason to believe that you have been causing a nuisance to a member of the public, Emma Holden, including following her and sending communications that could be construed as being menacing in nature. This is an informal warning on our part to stop doing this. We will be monitoring the situation carefully, and have asked Emma to report any further suspicious behaviour to us immediately, in which case we will take stronger action. Do you understand? . . . That's very sensible. I hope we don't need to speak about this again. Goodbye.'

'Well?' Emma said, as he ended the call. 'What did he say?'

Dan placed the phone on the table. 'He said that he was sorry, and that he'd stop doing what he'd been doing. I think it worked.'

28

Emma woke with a start. She'd been having another nightmare – it had been the wedding dream again. It had just got to the part where Dan had morphed into Stephen. He had smiled and gazed fondly into her eyes. This time, he had handed her an envelope: the package given to her in the deli café by Charlotte, Stuart's sister.

You really need to read this.

She had just slid a finger under the seal when a noise had woken her up.

Dan was moving quickly around the bedroom. 'Someone's knocking at the front door,' he said, pulling on his trousers and hunting out a shirt. 'I was just getting out of the shower. It's only seven thirty.'

Emma swung her legs out of bed and hastily wriggled into some clothes as Dan moved into the hallway. 'Who is it?' she heard him say. He came back into the room, looking worried. 'There's a man outside. You think I should open up?'

Again the person knocked.

Emma thought quickly. They needed to be careful, particularly under the current circumstances. 'Only on the security chain – don't open it fully.'

They both moved into the hallway.

Emma spoke through the door. 'Who's there?'

She looked through the spyhole, recognising the visitor just as he replied. 'My name's Scott Goulding. I'm here to explain, and apologise.'

Emma and Dan looked at each another, asking the same question with their eyes. Again, Emma looked through the spyhole. Now Scott was standing further back from the door, his hands on his hips, looking towards the floor. 'Let's open it,' she whispered to Dan. After a second, he nodded.

'Thanks, thanks,' Scott said, as Dan opened the door. He had his hands up, as if offering his surrender. 'I really need to explain everything.'

Dan stepped across his path as Emma retreated into the flat. 'Wait a second. If we let you in here, you don't try anything, okay?'

'Of course I won't.' Scott held up his hands again. 'I'm here to make peace, not cause any more trouble.'

They let him inside and into the kitchen. 'Take a seat,' Dan said.

Scott sat down at the table, but Emma and Dan remained standing. Up close, the profile of Scott Goulding's face was indeed reminiscent of Stephen Myers: the same hollow cheeks and pointed nose. His hair was the same shade of dark brown as Stephen Myers', but now, close up, it looked dyed. But his skin wasn't acne-scarred at all. Emma felt herself sinking back into confusion. Scott's green eyes, however, were also a perfect likeness of those of her one-time stalker, but he could have been wearing coloured contact lenses.

'Go on, then,' said Dan. 'You said you wanted to explain things.'

'I'm . . . well, you know, my name is Scott Goulding, and I'm . . . an actor.'

Emma watched, her back against the breakfast bar as Scott seemed to struggle for the right words. He looked genuinely embarrassed, maybe even a little scared. So much so that her fear of him dissipated immediately, and she began to feel sorry for him.

He looked up at her. 'I've been following you for the past couple of weeks.'

'Pretending to be Stephen Myers,' Emma said. 'Why?'

He shook his head, as if lamenting his actions. 'I did it because someone asked me to.'

Emma hadn't expected that. 'What?'

He looked her squarely in the eyes. 'Somebody asked me to follow you, and pretend to be Stephen Myers.'

'Who?' Dan said. 'Who asked you to do this?'

'I don't know.'

He didn't believe that. 'You must know.'

'I don't, I don't,' Scott protested. 'The person contacted me three weeks ago, via my website. Then they communicated via an anonymous email account. They've never told me their name, I swear.'

'And they asked you to follow me, impersonating Stephen Myers?' Emma asked.

'Yes.'

'But why?' Dan asked. 'Why did they want you to do it? And why did you go along with it?'

'They said they were auditioning people for a TV programme about you,' he said to Emma. 'And they wanted me to act the part of Stephen Myers, to see if I was suitable to take on that particular role.'

Dan and Emma exchanged glances. They both knew what the other was thinking.

Could it be—?

Emma was desperate to know more. 'So you went along with it, pretending to be Stephen Myers, following me around, scaring me at the Minack? That was you, wasn't it, in the toilets, standing outside the cubicle?'

'Yes,' he said, swallowing audibly. 'I followed you both to Cornwall. I stayed in a guest house just near your holiday apartment. I watched you on your trip to St Ives, took photos of you on the beach – just like I thought Stephen Myers would have done. And, yes, I was there at the theatre, and watched you go into the toilets. I wasn't planning to, but I followed you inside and stood next to your cubicle.'

'You really scared me,' Emma said.

'I know,' he said, shamefaced. 'I'm really sorry. It all got totally out of hand.' He decided he wouldn't mention just how far he'd gone at times.

'Was it you who paid for my meal in the café?'

'Yes. I was sitting across from you, on the other side of the room. I guess at the time, I thought it would be the kind of thing that Stephen Myers would do.'

'*Would* have done,' Dan said angrily. 'Stephen Myers is dead. You weren't just impersonating someone, you were playing their ghost.'

'I know.'

Dan continued. 'You sent the flowers too, with the message, "I'm still your number one fan"?'

Scott Goulding just nodded.

Dan wasn't finished. 'And was that you too, on the motorcycle, on the track leading to the vineyard?'

'Yes.'

'What were you planning to do there?' Dan pushed, as angry as Emma had ever seen him. 'Scare us? Or something more sinister?'

Scott looked shocked at the suggestion. 'No, of course not. I was just following you, watching, practising taking photos without you knowing.'

Dan shook his head. 'Pathetic.'

'You dressed like him,' Emma said. 'You even had the acne scarring – the girl in the florist's told us.'

'I know a make-up artist,' he explained. 'And the person who contacted me, they gave me details of what to wear, how to look. I looked just like him. I even went to see his mother, and she thought I *was* him – she actually thought I was Stephen Myers.' Just for a moment, did he look . . . *pleased* with himself? The look was short-lived, however. 'I really regret it now.'

'You went to see Mrs Myers?' Emma said.

'Yes. I'm not proud.'

Emma thought about Margaret Myers. The poor woman was already delusional; something like that could tip her over the edge.

That was so cruel.

'How did you know where we were?' she asked, turning her attention back to his actions against them. 'How did you know we were in Cornwall, staying at those apartments?'

'The person told me. They told me exactly where to go.'

'But how did they know?' Even as Emma asked that question, the thought that had first occurred to her in Cornwall returned – maybe it was someone close. *How many people knew about our holiday destination?* Again they were those who she trusted the most – Lizzy, Will, her father and, of course, Dan. She shook off the thought – none of them would have betrayed her, of that she was sure.

Scott offered no answers. 'I don't know, honestly. They would just send me an email, from an anonymously addressed Outlook account – all jumbled letters and numbers – with the instructions and the script.'

'The script?' This was getting even more bizarre.

'Yes, there was a script. I acted out the script, although I also did some improvisation. I'm really sorry – as I say, it all got totally out of hand. It's just been so difficult for me for the past few years, struggling to get work, going from one bit part to another. I've had to do bar jobs just to pay the rent, and the flat I live in, it's just terrible. They were offering me a chance, and I took it, but then it all became much more serious than I wanted. And now the police are involved – they called me last night. Please, I'm so sorry. Can you just let it drop?'

There was a long pause.

'As long as you leave Emma alone,' Dan said.

Scott's relief was palpable. 'Yes, of course I will. I promise this is the end of it. I don't want this any more. Stephen Myers, it was like he was taking possession of me. I don't want to ever think of him again. This is where it ends.'

'It had better be,' Dan replied. 'Otherwise the police are definitely going to want to speak to you again.'

'I know, I know. But I swear, no more. I'm really sorry.'

She didn't know why, but Emma believed him.

*   *   *

After Scott Goulding left, Emma paced up and down in the hallway, thinking about what had just been said. 'Making a production about me, auditioning for the part of Stephen Myers, using a script – it's got to be them, surely.'

Dan nodded. Emma could see he was still angry. 'Firework Films.'

29

'Are you sure you don't want me to call in sick?' Dan asked, as he stood up from the table at half past eight, dressed in his shirt and suit, his work bag slung over his shoulder. 'I will do, gladly, if you want me to be around today. The guys can do without me for a bit.'

Emma shook her head, touching Dan's arm. 'No, you go in. I'll be okay, honestly.'

He didn't look convinced. 'Are you sure?'

'Definitely.' Emma didn't want Dan to miss work. Despite what he had said about his colleagues being able to do without him, she knew that he had an important project on, for a key client, so it wouldn't make sense to risk ruining that. Not when the mystery of the Stephen Myers impersonator had been solved.

'Okay,' he said, 'but if anything happens, if Scott Goulding contacts you again, you've got to call me right away.'

'I will. '

'And if he comes calling, *don't* let him in. I know he sounded repentant, and said all the right things, but he might have a change of heart.'

Dan was right – Scott Goulding had been convincing, but who was to tell whether he was really telling the truth? For that reason, they had decided that they had to tell the police what had happened, including admitting that they had pretended to be the police on the phone to Scott. So, just a few minutes after Scott had left, they had called DS Loughlin and reported him. She had promised to pay him a visit, and warn him about his future conduct.

Emma did have a slight worry, however, that it might be counterproductive and risk antagonising him. 'You're right. If he comes back, I definitely won't be letting him in.'

'Good. I know this is probably the end of it, but I just don't want us to take any chances.'

They kissed.

Emma smiled as they pulled back from their embrace. 'Me, neither.'

After Dan had left for the office, Emma called Lizzy and Will and explained what had happened. Will was preparing for the parachute jump, and sounded really nervous. But Lizzy had a free day, so promised to call over later that morning.

'How about we go to Firework Films, and have it out with them?' Lizzy said during the call.

'We've decided that the best thing is to move on,' Emma said. 'Just walk away.'

There was a strong rationale for their decision not to tackle the company. Even if Firework Films was behind what had happened with Scott Goulding, there was little that Emma or Dan could do apart from complain to the company itself. It seemed implausible that the police would put resources into investigating it, as no crime had been committed.

Earlier, Dan had posed the question another way: 'If we cause a fuss with Firework Films, what good would it do us?'

'Make us feel better?' Emma had replied.

'Maybe it will give us short-term satisfaction,' he said, 'but will we win in the long term?'

'How do you mean?'

'Well, if we make a fuss, go in there causing trouble, making threats, they might want to take revenge – and they'll have the perfect opportunity to do just that.'

Suddenly Emma realised what he was getting at. 'The docudrama?'

'Yes. If that programme goes ahead, they can spin it any way they like. They might make us look bad – portray us in a bad light. I don't know how, but we've seen what their programmes can be like. Who's to say that they won't produce something that distorts the truth and twists the facts?'

'You really think that they might do that?'

'I don't know. But I'll tell you one thing for certain – I don't want to take any chances.'

Lizzy too had been convinced by Dan's argument, even though she hated the idea of letting them get away with their actions. 'But they'll get their comeuppance,' Lizzy finished. 'One day, they'll have to answer for the way they behave. I just hope that when they do, we get to hear about it.'

Emma changed into her running gear. She hadn't been for a run since the trip to Cornwall, and now she longed to stretch her legs and push her body physically.

The air was cooler than it had been of late, with more of a breeze, although it was still sunny. On the mid-October day, she could feel autumn coming and the leaves were beginning to fall from the trees.

As she pounded down Marylebone High Street towards Regent's Park, she considered the current situation. It did feel as if she had finally reached the light at the tunnel's end: they had successfully smoked out the stalker, revealing him to be far less threatening than they had all feared; and they'd uncovered the plot against them by the production company. They had taken these people on, and won. It felt good.

Once in the park she stepped up the pace, powering past the other joggers and dog walkers, feeling her legs burn as she reached the summit of Primrose Hill. There she stopped and admired the view. It seemed a lifetime ago that David Sherborn, masquerading as Eric, had approached her on that very spot. Yet it was only a little over a month ago.

Hands on her hips, she caught her breath. As she gazed at the London skyline, her thoughts turned to her father. He was out there, somewhere. She had every right to be angry with him, but she just felt sad. She pulled out her mobile and dialled his number once again. As with the other times, it went straight through to the answer service.

'Dad, please come home. We're not angry at you about anything. We just want you back here. I need you. We've rearranged the wedding for next week. I really want you to be there to give me away. You *have* to be there.'

She cut the call and dropped the phone back into the pocket of her tracksuit. The lie about the rearrangement of her and Dan's postponed wedding had been a spur-of-the-moment act designed to succeed where her past pleas had failed. But, now that she had said it, she longed for it to be true. She still felt it had been the right decision to wait until things had settled down before getting married, but the reality of the situation was that the date they had originally set their hearts on – the date that Emma had etched into her consciousness as her Wedding Day – had *not* been that special day.

Emma sighed. Maybe once the wedding happened, her recurring nightmare of her at the altar would also stop.

You really need to read this.

The words swam up from her subconscious. Stuart Harris's letter – it was still hidden in her sock drawer. She exhaled again and looked up at the sky. A plane cruised overhead, high in the blue.

Maybe she *should* open it.

Setting off back down the hill, now running even faster than before, she was unable to shake the idea from her thoughts.

30

'Hey.' Lizzy smiled as Emma answered the door. They hugged and Lizzy stepped into the flat. 'I hope you've got the kettle on, because I could really do with a drink – I meant to pick up a coffee on the way.'

'You didn't have to hurry, you know. I'm okay, honestly.'

'I know,' Lizzy said, closing the door behind her, 'but I wanted to.'

She followed Emma through into the kitchen. 'Anyway, the kettle's just boiling now,' Emma said. 'Perfect timing.'

'Great. So, how are you?'

'I'm fine.' It was an hour after she had returned from the run. In that time, she had showered, using it as an opportunity to consider more about whether she should open the letter from Stuart. She was becoming more convinced that she would, even going as far as getting it out of the drawer before putting it back again. But to open it still felt like a betrayal of Dan – as if she was once again reaching out to Stuart, behind his back.

'It's amazing that Scott Goulding just turned up like that and admitted everything. Dan's fake police call must have really spooked him.'

'It did.' Emma poured the boiling water into the teapot.

'You think this is the end of it?'

Emma nodded. 'I think so. I think Scott's days as a Stephen Myers impersonator are over. It sounds like he got caught up in something that got more serious than he expected. He's just desperate to get a break in the business, and for him, it made perfect sense. Even though to us, we can see how bad an idea it was.'

'He really seemed sorry then?'

'Yes, he did. I believed him when he said he said he was sorry.'

'Thank goodness for that. To be honest, Em, I was so relieved when you told me who had been doing this, and why. It just made it all feel so much less sinister.'

'I agree.' But Emma's response was preoccupied as she looked off towards the doorway to the bedroom.

'You sure you're okay?' Lizzy quizzed. 'You look like you're worrying about something.'

Emma smiled ruefully. 'You know me too well. I nearly opened Stuart's letter before.'

'Oh, right. What stopped you?'

'I don't know. I guess maybe I'm scared of what it's going to say.'

'I can totally understand that. But you do want to open it, don't you?' Lizzy looked at her friend with concern.

'Why do you say that?'

'Because I know that you did care about Stuart, and you wouldn't want to deny him his chance to say goodbye.'

Emma closed her eyes. 'I feel as though if I did open it, I'd be cheating on Dan.'

'But it wouldn't be like that, Em.'

'I know, but that's how it feels.' She swallowed. 'You didn't see him, over the weekend in St Ives, when he was talking about how he felt about everything. He was so hurt at what happened between me and Stuart that night on the boat.'

'But nothing *did* happen.'

'I know nothing happened in that way, but just the fact that we were together, while Dan was missing, you know . . . It really got to him. I don't think he was jealous. I think it just made him really sad. We've got over it, talked it through, and I just don't want to risk jeopardising that by doing something unnecessary.'

'Then don't open it. Let me do it. Where is it?'

'In my sock drawer, by the bed.'

Lizzy got up from the table. Emma could see she was in one of her determined moods. 'Lizzy!' But she was already heading for the bedroom.

'Now,' she said, returning with the letter in hand, 'shall I open it?'

Emma gazed at the letter. If she didn't open it, she might always wonder what was inside. After a second she nodded, pushing aside her doubts.

'This will be part of moving on,' Lizzy said, starting to tear along the top. 'Closing that chapter in your life and starting afresh.'

Emma didn't feel anything like certain about this. But Lizzy was right – if she didn't open the letter, how would she ever truly be able to move on? There would always be that thought of what had Stuart said. And yes, deep down, she did want to give Stuart his opportunity to say what he wanted to.

Lizzy opened the envelope and pulled out a photograph. As she examined it, her forehead creasing, Emma bent over, picking up a piece of paper that had fallen from the envelope onto the floor. She read the handwritten message.

I knew you wouldn't be able to resist. Just wanted to show you how happy my brother was with his fiancée Sally before you came back on the scene and ruined it all.

Emma felt numb.

Fiancée? Stuart hadn't told her about that.

'I don't believe it,' Lizzy said, still examining the photo. 'Tell me that's not who I think it is.' She passed it to Emma. Stuart was smiling at the camera, his arm around a girl, who was also smiling broadly.

It was Sally – Stuart's fiancée. But they knew her by a different name: Amy, Will's new girlfriend.

Part Four

31

Will took a gulp from his second coffee of the day, before pacing into the bathroom and looking in the mirror. 'You can do this, you can do it.' He didn't feel entirely convinced. In fact, first thing that morning, he had nearly called Amy to postpone the jump. He'd thought up some pathetic excuse – he was feeling slightly unwell, so it was best to wait until he was 100 per cent – but, ultimately, he'd resisted calling her and instead tried some self-motivational techniques he'd once read about in a magazine in the dentist's waiting room.

It was now twelve thirty. Amy would be arriving in half an hour to drive them to the airfield. Then there would be no going back. She would offer him a get-out, that was certain, but he wouldn't be able to take it.

He spent the next twenty-five minutes listening to his favourite rock tracks, turning the volume up so loud that at first he didn't hear Amy's knock. When he realised she had arrived, he scrambled for the volume control and raced towards the door.

'Hey,' Amy said with a smile. 'I thought you were ignoring me.'

'No, no, of course not.' Will felt much more out of breath than he should have been.

'So, are you ready?'

He swallowed his nerves. 'Yes, I'm ready.'

'I don't understand this,' Emma said, staring at the photograph. 'The girl Will is going out with was Stuart's fiancée? And she's pretending to be someone else?'

'Are we sure it's the same person?'

The question had to be asked, but it was clear – the girl in the photograph was the same girl whom Will was dating. Although the time they had met her – in the foyer of Selfridges – had been brief, there was no mistaking her. After all, both had been scrutinising Will's new flame closely. 'We both know it's her, don't we?'

Lizzy nodded. 'Then what do we do?'

Emma shook her head. *What is all this about?* 'Well, we've got to tell Will, of course. But I've got to tell him in the right way. You know how he feels about her – he's in love. The other day he told me she's the best thing that's ever happened to him. So it's going to devastate him when he finds out who she really is, and that she's been lying.'

'I know. I just don't get it, Em. What is this woman doing? What's her agenda?'

'I've got no idea, but I know someone who might be able to shed some light on it all.'

'Who's that?'

'Charlotte, Stuart's sister.'

Lizzy nodded. 'So we speak to her first, and then decide how to break the news to Will?'

'I think it's all we can do. We need to try and find out more about who she is before we do anything else.'

'But Charlotte Harris . . .' Lizzy paused. 'Well, she's not exactly on friendly terms with you. What she did – giving you the photograph, pretending it was from Stuart, and the note she wrote with it . . . it's pretty nasty. She might refuse to talk to us.'

'She might, but I don't think so. I think she wants to tell me more, for me to ask about what happened. Maybe the photograph was bait.'

'You think she knows that this girl is seeing Will?'

'No idea, but we need to find out.'

32

'I knew you wouldn't be able to resist opening the letter.' Charlotte Harris took a seat opposite Emma and Lizzy in the same deli café where they'd met before. Emma had been right – she had been more than happy to meet them – and just an hour after the initial call, there they were, face to face.

Emma looked at her closely. She was trying to look triumphant, but behind that bravado Emma could sense something else – sadness, possibly. Her face seemed tense, her eyes reddened.

'Why did you do it, Charlotte?' asked Emma.

'As I said,' said Charlotte slowly, 'I wanted you to know how happy my brother was before you came back on the scene.'

'You make it sound like it was my decision to come back into Stuart's life. But it wasn't. It was the other way round.'

Charlotte looked affronted. 'You led him on.'

'I didn't. I really didn't. As I explained to you before, I didn't lead him on.'

Again, this didn't look like the answer Charlotte wanted to hear.

'He didn't tell me that he was engaged,' Emma insisted. 'He mentioned he'd been seeing somebody, but he made out that it wasn't serious.'

Charlotte snorted. 'Wasn't serious? They were due to get married *today*!'

Emma was stunned. 'What? Today was supposed to be their wedding day?'

'Yes. It had been planned for almost two years. So all that time you were with Stuart, Sally was looking forward to what should have been the best day of her life. When Stuart died it totally devastated her. It's devastated us all, but for her it's worse – Stuart was her future. And that died too, along with my brother. Now she feels like she has nothing to live for.'

'I'm really sorry for her. I am.'

'Two days after Stuart died, she tried to take an overdose. The only reason she didn't succeed is because I happened to go round to her flat and find her just a few minutes after she'd taken the tablets. The hospital staff saved her.'

Emma thought back to the girl that Will had introduced them to. The confident, energetic, happy girl called Amy. She didn't bear any resemblance to the Sally that Charlotte was describing. For a second it made her question again whether the two girls were indeed the same person. But there was no doubt.

It was time to ask the question. 'Do you know that Sally is dating my brother?'

Charlotte looked genuinely shocked, and then disbelieving. 'You're lying.'

'I'm not.'

'It's true,' Lizzy added. 'The girl in the photograph with Stuart, she's the girl that Will is going out with.'

Charlotte was silent.

'She said her name was Amy,' Emma continued. 'None of us had any idea who she really was until we saw the photograph this morning.'

'I don't understand,' said Charlotte finally. 'She did have a sister called Amy, but she died when she was a baby. Why would she—?'

'We thought you might know,' Emma said. 'We thought you might be able to explain what was going on.'

Charlotte put a hand to her head. 'Why would she date your brother, why?' She shook her head, bewildered.

Emma tried a different tack. 'Tell me about Sally. She said to Will that she's a sports teacher at a comprehensive school. Is that right?'

'Yes, yes, that's right.'

'And she's very adventurous – travelling, skydiving, things like that.'

'Yes, she is. For their honeymoon, they were going to go to Nepal, trekking in the mountains; it was going to be wonderful – a real adventure. Stuart had been really looking forward to it.'

'How did they meet?'

'At a screenwriting course. Stuart wanted to expand his options, you know, from just acting to working more behind the scenes, too.'

A sickening realisation suddenly hit Emma. 'Sally is a screenwriter?'

'Yes. She's had a few things on the radio – plays and sketches, but she always wanted to go into television and film. It just hasn't happened for her yet.'

I acted out the script. Emma remembered something that Scott Goulding had said.

Sally wrote scripts.

Emma turned to Lizzy. 'Will knew we were going to Cornwall, and he also knew about Windsor. If he'd mentioned it to Sally, then she would have been able to pass that information on to Scott Goulding, telling him where to go. And she wrote the scripts that he had to act out.'

'What's going on?' Charlotte asked. 'I don't understand.'

'I'm only beginning to understand it myself. We need to call Will.'

She pulled her mobile out of her pocket, but before she could dial Will, it rang. She didn't recognise the number.

'Emma. It's Scott Goulding. This morning I got an email from the person, and I thought I needed to tell you about it. The message is really weird.'

'Go on.'

'They thanked me for my work, but said they would no longer require my services because I'm not involved in the final scene, a double suicide, which is being shot today. That's all it said.'

Emma cut off the call, waves of sickness swelling and rolling inside her. This time she dialled Will, her fingers shaking.

Lizzy saw the horror in her friend's face. 'What is it, Em? What's happened?'

Will wasn't answering.

'It's Will,' she said. 'I think she's planning to kill him.'

'*What?*'

'The tandem parachute jump. I think she's planning to commit suicide, and take Will with her.'

33

'How are you feeling?' Amy asked as they approached the airfield. 'Are you still sure you want to go through with this?'

Will was staring out of the car window, looking at the strip of tarmac that would be their launching point. He'd felt better, but Amy's relaxed manner helped him contain his nerves. After all, he would be strapped to her the whole time – she was the one who would be dictating everything: the timing and execution of the jump, the opening of the parachute, the direction of their descent and the landing. All he had to do was enjoy the ride. 'I'm fine,' he said eventually. 'I still want to do it.'

'Good, that's good.'

Will thought about sending a text message to Emma – not really a goodbye message, but you never knew, did you? But he couldn't find his mobile. He must have left it at home.

They turned left through the entrance and up the main drive-way to a small car park, where only three other vehicles were parked. The airfield wasn't much more than the take-off and landing area. Will could see only a single plane – a flimsy-looking craft that didn't fill him with confidence. There was a small, prefabricated building in front of them, which looked like something from a prisoner-of-war camp.

'That's where the briefing room is,' Amy explained, yanking up the handbrake. 'There are also changing rooms and toilets.'

'I'll need the toilets, probably more than once,' Will joked as he undid his seat belt. The next strap that would be wrapped around him wouldn't be so familiar.

He expected Amy to laugh, but she didn't.

'You ready then?' she asked.

Suddenly she seemed so serious. But that was probably a good thing.

If you're going to put your life in the hands of someone else, surely it's better if that person is taking things seriously and being professional about it all.

Inside the building they were greeted by a tall, well-built man about Will's age. 'This is Harvey,' Amy said. 'He'll be flying the plane.'

'Pleased to meet you.' Harvey held out a large hand.

'You, too.' Will's hand was shaking as he brought it up to greet him.

'So I hear this is your first time doing a jump?'

Will nodded.

'Don't worry,' Harvey said, 'it'll be absolutely fine. You're in safe hands, I promise. I've been doing this for years, and my colleague here, she's a fantastic instructor and jumper.'

'Good, that's good.'

For the next fifteen minutes, Amy talked Will through the pre-jump training. Again, her professional persona had taken over, and there was no room for informal chat. They covered all the necessary issues, which most importantly included how to touch down safely. It was the one part of the jump where Will had to ensure that he positioned himself correctly, rather than merely relying on Amy. She also talked him through exactly what would happen, in what order, from take-off to landing. There would be no surprises.

Will watched Amy as they changed into their suits. 'Thank you. For making me feel so good.'

Amy looked up. 'Don't mention it. I do this all the time. You get to know how to give people the power to enjoy it.'

'No, I don't mean about the jump,' he said. 'I mean about everything.'

'Right.'

'I mean, I know we've only known each other for a few weeks, but you've totally transformed my life. I was in such a bad place before you came along. But now, I just feel – well, I feel *alive*. And it's all because of you, because of how amazing you are. I really do think you've changed me for the better, for ever.'

Amy's smile seemed tinged with sadness. 'I'm glad, Will. That's a really lovely thing of you to say.'

'I know it's early days,' Will continued. 'But I really think that this is the start of something really special.' He looked at her for some sign. 'At least, I hope it is.'

Amy just looked at him.

Seeing her reaction, Will regretted saying that. 'I'm sorry – I'm coming on too strong, aren't I? I don't want to scare you off.'

She came over and hugged him, then kissed him softly on the cheek. 'You're a good man, Will. Don't forget it.'

Then she went back to preparing her gear.

34

'It's there!' Emma shouted. 'Just up ahead.'

It had taken them nearly an hour to reach the airfield, speeding most of the way. Thank goodness Will had told Emma the previous night where the parachute jump was taking place. A quick check on the internet for directions, and they'd sped off in Lizzy's car, picking up Dan en route. The journey had been torturous. Will still wasn't answering his phone, and the number for the airfield didn't work. They'd left messages on the phones of DI Gasnier and PC Loughlin, unable to reach them directly.

Emma craned her neck in an attempt to spot the plane. 'Please, please, I hope we're not too late.'

'I can't see anything in the air,' Dan said from the back seat.

Emma couldn't see anything, either. The sky was clear – if the plane was already airborne, surely they would be able to see it? 'Please, God, don't let anything happen to him.'

'The entrance is there, on the left!' Dan shouted.

They turned a hard, fast left through the entrance and Lizzy stepped on the accelerator, powering towards the car park.

It was then that they saw a plane emerge from behind the small outbuilding, taxiing down the runway. It was moving away from them, and it was impossible to see who was on board.

'We're too late!' Emma cried. 'Quick, stop the car, stop the car!'

Lizzy pulled up sharply and Emma threw open the door, sprinting across the gravel and grass towards the wire mesh fence that separated them from the airstrip. 'Stop! Stop!' She clung to the fence as if for support.

Dan and Lizzy came up beside her at a run. They all watched as the plane moved even further away, gaining speed down the runway. Then it took to the air, banking right as it rose into the clear, blue sky.

Emma broke down in tears.

They were too late.

35

They watched, stunned, as the plane continued to climb. Emma felt sick. Was she really going to watch Will plummet to his death?

Maybe there was still a chance. She wiped away the tears and looked over at the building. 'There must be someone in there. Maybe they can contact the pilot.'

'You're right,' Dan said, already moving. 'They must have some form of ground control.'

The three of them raced into the building.

The first person they saw was Will. He was sitting on a bench, his head hung low.

'Will!' Emma shouted. 'You're okay!'

Will looked up, shocked by their sudden appearance. 'Of course I am. Why shouldn't I be?'

Emma embraced him. 'You didn't go up in the plane!'

'I was about to. But at the last moment she said I couldn't do it.' He looked totally destroyed. 'We were almost ready to get on the plane, but Amy told me she wanted to do it on her own. I don't know why. Maybe it was what I said. Maybe I scared her off.' He looked at Emma. 'Maybe she's trying to tell me it's over.'

'She must have decided not to go through with it,' Emma said, her knees weak. 'She decided she couldn't do it.'

'What? What's this all about? Why are you all here?'

'We came to save you,' Lizzy said.

'*Save* me?'

'We'll explain later,' Dan said urgently. 'Is there somebody here in charge of ground control? There's still time to stop this.'

'Of course,' Emma said, remembering that this wasn't over yet. 'We've got to stop her from jumping.'

Despite his confusion, Will ran with it. 'There are two guys in the next room. They've got radio contact with the plane. Amy told me they need to be in touch in case of any problems.'

They all headed through the door, not bothering to knock. Two older men were sitting at a communication desk, drinking tea, listening to the radio. They nearly spilt their drinks as the four of them burst in. 'Hey, what do you think you're—?'

'Call the plane back down,' Dan shouted. 'Now.'

'She's planning to kill herself,' Emma explained. 'She's not going to open her parachute.'

'It's okay,' Lizzy said to Will, who looked horrified. 'She'll be okay.'

The men didn't touch the radio. They simply sat and stared.

'Please,' Emma pleaded. 'Please, just call the plane down.'

The men exchanged glances. 'Do it, Bob,' one of them said. 'Call them back.'

They put out the call over the radio for the plane to return to base immediately. There was no explanation given, and none asked for. A few minutes later, the plane touched down on the runway.

They were waiting for Sally – Amy as they had known her – as she re-entered the changing area. She looked pale. 'What was all that abou—?' Her face fell when she saw the welcoming party. She focused her attention on Will. 'You know, don't you?'

Will nodded, white as a sheet himself. 'What . . . what changed your mind?'

She pinched the bridge of her nose, closing her eyes, and seemed to sway slightly. 'You did, Will. What you said, about me changing your life. And about how amazing I was. I couldn't do it.'

They both had tears in their eyes. Will moved towards her, but she backed off, as if she was afraid to be touched.

Will shook his head in disbelief. 'It was all an act?'

'I'm sorry.'

'You never really felt anything for me?' His voice took on a hollow tone. 'You were just using me, fattening me up like an animal before slaughter?'

'This was all to punish me, wasn't it?' Emma said, stepping forward and putting a hand on Will's arm. 'You blame me for Stuart's death, just like Charlotte does, and you wanted to punish me. You arranged for Scott Goulding to act the part of Stephen Myers, to scare me.' She stared at the woman before her, uncomprehendingly. 'How did you know him? Was it through Guy Roberts?'

'No,' Sally replied. She took a deep breath. 'Stuart knew him. I knew he'd do it, because he's so desperate for work.'

'So you contacted him, pretending to be from a production company, and asked him to follow me.'

'Yes.'

'But why target Will, too?'

Sally couldn't meet her eye. 'Because I wanted to take something precious away from you, just like you took it away from me!' And she broke down in tears, sliding down against the wall, hiding her head in her hands.

The group looked on in silence.

'I'm really sorry for what's happened to you,' Emma said. 'I really am.'

'Today was our wedding day,' Sally sobbed. 'I don't know what to do. I'm so sorry.'

'I know . . . I know.' And Emma found herself moving forward and putting an arm around her.

36

Police arrived at the airfield twenty minutes later. They spoke briefly to the group, getting the basic facts of what had happened, and then told them they could go. Sally, who had now calmed down, was taken in for questioning.

Back at Emma and Dan's flat, the four friends found someone waiting at the front door.

It was Edward Holden.

'I've been so stupid, Emma. And I'm so sorry, I really am. Did you mean what you said about still wanting me to give you away?'

'Of course!' Emma embraced him. 'I couldn't get married without you.'

'Thank you,' he said, resting his head against her hair. 'You don't know how happy that makes me feel.' He pulled back. 'I've got some other good news. My solicitor just called, and they've dropped the prosecution.'

'That's brilliant news! But why?'

'I don't know exactly. He said something about the police not following due process with the investigation. I have to go and see him tomorrow and he'll explain it all then.'

'That's great, Dad.' Will placed a hand on his shoulder. 'It's all over then.'

Emma nodded, relief flooding through her. 'It's the end of it all.'

'Well, not quite,' Dan said, slowly. Emma looked at him, unsure of his expression. 'There's definitely one piece of unfinished business.' He looked at her, seriously. 'Em, I never did get a chance in Cornwall to tell you about my surprise . . .'

37

Emma Holden – now Emma Carlton – stood on the stage of the Minack Theatre in her stunning white wedding dress. The weather had been extremely kind for early November, and it was sunny and mild, with just a gentle breeze coming off the water. As the photographer, a local man with a fantastic reputation, clicked away, Emma felt like a million dollars.

She couldn't stop smiling.

'Could you just turn a little to your left, and hold the bouquet slightly higher?' Emma raised the bouquet of fresh pink roses. 'That's it, great.'

It had been a perfect day. First the wedding service at a beautiful village chapel just five miles down the coast, and then straight to the Minack for the photo shoot. It was rare for the venue to allow wedding photographs to be taken, and normally it was reserved for locals, so Emma felt especially privileged to have the opportunity. Dan had persuaded the owners – Emma's background in theatre had helped.

Dan had sorted out everything. Not just the chapel and the theatre photo-shoot, but also accommodation for the guests and the reception in a hotel overlooking the bay at St Ives.

While the photographer reviewed his latest shots on his digital camera, Emma took the opportunity to look up towards the top of the amphitheatre, where the guests were mingling, drinks in hand. She saw Dan talking to Richard and Will, and Lizzy chatting with Miranda and her father. Lizzy spotted her looking and waved.

'I think we'll have some of you and your closest friends now,' the photographer said. 'If you'd like to call them down, that would be great.'

Emma caught Lizzy's eye again and beckoned her down. 'Tell Dan and Will to come too,' she shouted.

The four of them laughed and joked as the photographer readied himself.

'I understand now what you mean about this place,' Lizzy said. 'It would be so amazing to perform here.'

'Maybe we should both do it,' Emma replied. 'After we've got tired of the London theatre scene.'

Just one week earlier, Emma had landed herself a wonderful agent, who had immediately sent her for an audition for a fantastic part, playing the lead role in a dramatic new stage play about a family emigrating to Australia. Emma felt quietly confident about her chances. It felt right to move away from TV and film, and she was really excited about the possibility of starting a new chapter in her professional as well as personal life.

'I'm so pleased for you, Em. You've had such a difficult time, it's great that everything's now going so well.'

'Hey, concentrate, you two,' Dan exclaimed. 'This poor guy is trying to get your attention!'

They faced forward and posed for the camera as the photographer fired off another round of shots.

'So, Mrs Carlton, is this a good surprise or what?' Dan said, kissing Emma on the cheek and looping an arm around her waist.

'It's a *fantastic* surprise, Mr Carlton.'

'Well, how would you like another?'

'If it's as good as this one, then I wouldn't say no.'

'Oh, it is.' He smiled. 'How about a honeymoon on a tropical paradise island?'

'You're joking.'

'Would I?'

'Then where?'

'Mauritius. We fly out in two weeks. I've already cleared it with work.'

'That's, well, I'm speechless!'

'You'll have to thank your dad, because he's contributed half the cost. Now his business is back in rude health, he said it was the least he could do.'

'Wow. I will.' Emma looked up and saw her father smiling, his arm around Miranda. She'd not seen him this happy for a long time.

'Will's also given us some spending money as his wedding present.'

Emma leant over and kissed Will. 'Thanks.'

'Don't mention it.'

'No, really, thanks. How's Katie enjoying the day?'

'Great, it seems to be going great.' Will had surprised everyone by announcing that he had asked an old school friend to be his plus one. Emma knew that, although they had never dated, he had been close to Katie Jones for years, before losing touch when everyone went to university. Just one week ago they had had a chance meeting at Euston Station, and had got on as well as ever. Will, with his newfound confidence, had invited Katie to Cornwall for the celebrations, and she had accepted.

'That's fantastic, Will,' said Emma. 'You really deserve to be happy.'

'I just hope Amy – I mean, Sally – is okay,' he said. 'And I hope one day she meets the right person.'

'It sounds like she's getting the best support now, from what the police said.'

'Yes, that's good.' Will nodded, and turned away.

'Right, that's it,' the photographer said. 'I've got all I need from here. You're free to return to your guests.'

Emma, Dan, Lizzy and Will made their way back up to the waiting crowd and collected glasses of champagne from one of the servers.

Emma raised her glass and smiled at her family and friends as they looked on. 'Here's to the beginning of a brighter future!'

It's not over…

Read on for the first two chapters of the thrilling final
instalment of the Emma Holden Trilogy.

The One You Trust

I

Lizzy paused as she arrived outside Dan and Emma's apartment building. The weather was that of a typical early December morning – sunny but bitterly cold. She had her hands buried deep inside her winter coat, her strawberry-blonde hair covered by a woolly hat. She liked this kind of weather – it was Christmassy, and she loved the festive season.

Lizzy took a deep breath as she considered the events of the past two weeks, a feeling of dread rising within her, but she entered the apartment block anyway, glancing over at the post trays where the postman deposited the mail for each resident.

There were several letters in the trays, including a variety of Friday's newspapers. Hesitating again, nerves tightening, she shook off the feeling of dread, knowing she had to face up to things.

She leafed quickly through the mail. Thankfully, there was nothing to be worried about there.

Not like nine days ago.

The first letter had been waiting for her three days after her best friend, Emma, and her new husband, Dan, had left for their honeymoon in Mauritius.

Emma had asked Lizzy if she would mind the flat while they were away. She had only asked Lizzy to pop around once in a while, just to check that all was well, but Lizzy had found herself drawn to the place every day. Maybe after all that had happened, she just felt the need to be extra vigilant. Even though the nightmare was over.

Or so they had all thought.

*   *   *

The grey envelope containing the letter had been the only thing in the post tray that third morning.

It had been addressed to Lizzy, sent externally, first-class post. Inside had been a piece of lined paper, with just a single, taunting, typed sentence, in a Gothic font, centred on the page.

Who can you really trust, Lizzy?

Lizzy had never considered herself easily intimidated: she had always been somewhat thick-skinned, a trait she'd developed during childhood years of being playfully taunted by two older brothers, and which had further hardened by surviving in the sometimes catty world of theatre. But this had certainly got to her; for the rest of the day it had remained uppermost in her mind. *Who sent this? And why?*

Whoever had sent it must have known that Emma and Dan were away, and that Lizzy was visiting the apartment building. She had found herself looking over her shoulder, wondering whether the person was watching, following.

But she had refused to be intimidated.

Defying her fears, Lizzy returned to the flat every day, making the post trays her first port of call. And, each day, she had expected to find another letter for her. But it had been another seven days before the next communication arrived. The modus operandi had been the same: a single typed sentence, in Gothic font, posted first class, addressed to her.

The one you trust is the one to fear. Who do you trust, Lizzy?

Lizzy had no idea what that was supposed to mean. It wasn't a threat, as such; it was more like a warning. But it was not a friendly warning – it was designed to unsettle her.

Again, the question is who ...

The suspect was obvious: Sally Thompson. Two months before, Sally, masquerading as a girl called Amy, had planned to kill Emma's brother, Will Holden. A qualified skydive instructor, she had met and dated him, all with the intention of tandem-jumping out of a plane with him – and sending them both to their deaths. The motive had been revenge on the family: Sally blamed Emma for the death of her fiancé, Stuart Harris, who killed himself after his advances towards

Emma, to whom he had once also been engaged, had been spurned. But, ultimately, Sally hadn't carried it through: she'd pulled back from the brink and hadn't, in fact, committed any crime. Which was why the police had only given her an official caution.

Maybe she was too obvious a suspect.

But if not Sally Thompson, then who?

Lizzy hadn't told anyone about the letters. She certainly wasn't going to let it spoil Dan and Emma's honeymoon. There was no way that she was going to let this individual ruin things. And she hadn't told Will, because she wasn't convinced that he would be able to keep quiet if Emma happened to get in touch. She knew he probably wouldn't say anything, but it wasn't worth the risk. Lizzy had considered contacting the police, but it was probably just some loser with nothing better to do, who had been attracted to the case following the press publicity.

Lizzy climbed the stairs to Emma and Dan's top-floor flat. She entered, glancing back down towards the staircase as she closed the door. There was – of course – nobody there.

Once inside, she did her daily check of each room, moving quickly. Everything was as it should be. But being in the place, devoid of its owners, unnerved her, and she never stayed for more than a minute or so, always glad to leave.

Lizzy peered around the bathroom door. Again, nothing. But, inside her head, she heard Will's voice.

It's Richard. I think he's dead.

That image, of Will emerging from the bathroom, blood all over his hands, having found the battered body of Dan's brother, Richard, still haunted her – even though she knew Richard was safely up in Edinburgh now, getting on with his life.

She always left the bathroom until last.

Lizzy shivered, locking the door and turning to go back down the stairs. It wasn't getting any easier, but she *was* going to come back every day until Dan and Emma returned. She wasn't going to let her fears get the better of her.

By the time she reached the hallway, she was feeling better. But the sight of a grey envelope in Dan and Emma's post tray stopped her dead.

She looked across at the external door. There was no one. Moving over to the tray, she took hold of the letter. It was the same type of washed out grey envelope as previously but, this time, no stamp.

It had been hand-delivered.

Lizzy gripped the envelope. 'They've been here, just now.'

She was startled by the sudden sound of the outside door swinging open. It was Emma's elderly downstairs neighbour.

'Oh, hello.' Mr Henderson looked surprised to see her, although she'd seen him a few times over the past few days and had explained that she was looking after the flat. She wondered whether he, like his wife, was starting to lose his memory.

'Did you see anyone leaving the apartments just now?' Lizzy asked.

He looked confused, clutching onto a couple of shopping bags.

Lizzy tried again. 'Did anyone pass you, just now, as you were coming in?'

'Yes,' he said, his face brightening a little. 'A man, I think.'

'You think?' Lizzy bit her lip with frustration. 'What did he look like?'

'I don't know,' he replied. 'He was wearing a hat. A cap, one of those peaked caps. Seemed to cover his face. He was looking down. I didn't see his face.'

'Do you know which way he went?'

'Towards Euston Road. Is he a friend of yours?'

'I don't think so,' Lizzy said. 'What colour cap?'

Mr Henderson thought for a moment. 'Blue.'

Lizzy pulled open the door, still holding the letter. 'Thanks, Mr Henderson.'

She stepped out onto the pavement and peered down the road. There were a few people walking towards her, and another several walking in the direction of Euston Road, some way up the street. One of them looked like they might be wearing a cap, but it was too far to tell.

Lizzy set off up the road after the distant figures, walking at a pace just short of a jog. She wasn't sure what she was going to do if one of them turned out to be the person in the cap, but she wanted to do something.

She passed two people – a twenty-something girl listening to music through headphones, and a businessman texting on his mobile phone. And then, further ahead, she saw someone else. Striding purposefully, wearing a blue cap.

'Hey, you!'

Lizzy wasn't sure why she shouted, but it certainly got their attention – and confirmed her suspicions that this was the person who'd left the letter.

They turned their head at a low angle, just enough to see Lizzy, but still shielding their face beneath the cap.

And then they ran.

Lizzy gave chase, but the individual in the cap was just too fast and rapidly increased the distance between them. If she had been Emma, Lizzy thought, then maybe she would have had a chance. But Lizzy, although relatively fit, wasn't naturally sporty, and didn't run for fun.

She didn't give up, though, and pursued the person up towards the busy Euston Road, sure that the traffic would slow their speed. But the person in the cap just sprinted straight across the road, dodging buses, taxis and cars, and carried on across into Regent's Park.

Lizzy could only stand by the kerb and watch from the other side, punching the crossing button repeatedly in a vain attempt to stop the traffic.

She leant against the roadside railings to catch her breath and only then remembered she still had the sealed letter in her hand. She tore it open.

This time it wasn't just a message.

'What the hell?' she said to herself.

2

'I can't believe that tomorrow is our last full day.'

'Me neither,' Dan said, as they sat down for dinner on the hotel's restaurant terrace. They were looking out over the stunning beach and a huge expanse of the Indian Ocean, bathed in a glorious sunset.

Emma closed her eyes and enjoyed the feel of the mild, strengthening breeze, which in the past hour had taken the edge off the humidity. Her skin had tanned a lovely golden colour since their arrival, bringing out the warm honey highlights in her dark brown hair. She reopened her eyes as Dan continued.

'It seems to have gone so quickly,' he said, subconsciously touching his dark hair, which he had cut shorter just before the trip. Emma liked the new style. 'Cheers to a wonderful honeymoon, Mrs Carlton.' He smiled and raised his glass of champagne to meet Emma's.

They'd come down early for the meal, before the later rush, so the restaurant was quiet, with only two other couples, seated some tables away. This dinner, in the smaller, Indian-themed restaurant, was a special treat arranged by Dan for the Friday night. Unlike the larger eating places in the hotel, he had had to book ahead, and the setting – for open-air dining by candlelight – was idyllic.

But, Emma thought, although this was an extra-special meal, in truth, everything about the holiday had been a treat. The hotel was amazing; it was a luxurious complex right by the best beach on Mauritius' east coast, complete with a number of swimming pools, several restaurants serving a vast array of food from around the world, and rooms that seemed palatial in their size and décor. And then there was the island itself. A real paradise, bathed in sunshine, and offering an intoxicating mix of cultures, sights and landscapes.

It was certainly the holiday of a lifetime.

'Em, are you okay?'

Emma snapped out of her daydream, releasing that she was absentmindedly twirling her hair around one finger. She smiled at her husband. 'I was just thinking, on Sunday we go back to reality. Back to London, the flat . . .'

'It's not that bad, you know,' Dan joked, his attention taken for a second by one of the small sparrows that spent each day squabbling over the crumbs that fell from the tables.

'No, it's not bad at all.' She tried to smile.

'Everything is going to be all right,' Dan said, reading her mind. He reached across the table top and took her hand. 'Everything is going to be absolutely fine.'

Emma went to say something, then paused.

'What is it?'

'I don't want to spoil tonight,' she replied. 'We shouldn't let anything spoil it.'

'I know. But' – Dan looked at her – 'if you're worried about something, then it might be better to just get it out. We all know what happens when people keep secrets.'

'Okay,' Emma said, nodding reluctantly. 'Okay, I'll tell you. But, please, I hope you won't be upset.'

'Of course I won't, Em.'

Emma sipped some champagne to ready herself. 'Last night, I had that dream again.'

'Right . . .' Dan knew just what she meant. 'The nightmare at the church altar.'

Emma nodded. 'It was exactly the same as the other times. I was standing next to you, we were getting married—'

'And then I turn into Stuart,' Dan interrupted.

'Yes. And then he turns into—'

'Stephen Myers.' Dan sighed as he thought back over recent events. Just over three months ago, Emma had discovered that

Stephen Myers, a man who had stalked her when she had worked as an actor on a soap opera in Manchester, had been murdered four years previously, by Stuart. Her brother, Will, had been pressured by Stuart to help him dispose of the body. And it had also resulted, this summer, in the kidnap of Dan by Stephen's father, Peter Myers, as he sought revenge on Emma and her family and friends.

Emma shook her head. 'I really thought that once everything was sorted ... you know, after the wedding, then it wouldn't happen. I thought it was in the past.'

Yet she knew that the situation that had given birth to the nightmare wasn't in the past at all. Peter Myers had yet to be sentenced, and there was still the worry that he would one day reveal that his son had been murdered, and Will's role in that.

And then there was the unanswered question. *How did Peter Myers find out that Stuart killed his son?*

Dan was about to reply but was interrupted by a waiter. 'Sir, madam – are you ready to order?'

Emma and Dan exchanged a glance.

'Not quite yet,' Dan said. 'Another couple of minutes?'

'Certainly,' the waiter replied, and moved away.

Dan turned back to Emma. 'Why would I be upset about you having a recurrent nightmare?'

Emma shrugged, shaking her head. 'Because this dream, it's coming from inside me. I'm creating it. Inside, I must still be thinking about Stuart Harris and Stephen Myers. Doesn't that bother you?'

Dan nodded, reflectively. 'Yes, it does. But not in the way you think. It bothers me because I want you to be free of the bad memories, free of the nightmares.'

'Thanks.'

He thought for a moment. 'Last night, is that the first time you've had the dream since the wedding?'

'Yes.'

'I thought you seemed a bit distant today. I could tell something was bothering you.'

They'd been on an all-day, escorted tour of the island. It had been a lovely day, but Dan was right – Emma had been distracted.

'Look,' Dan said. 'Maybe the dream is down to worry – worry about going home. This past two weeks, it's been an escape. I don't know about you, but everything about being here . . . well, it's felt a world away from all the bad things that have happened to us recently.'

'I'd hardly thought of any of it since we arrived,' Emma agreed. 'We've been too busy having fun. It just seemed like a distant memory – as if it happened to someone else.'

'Exactly. And now it's coming to an end, we have to go back home, to where it all happened. We have to face up to the fact that it did happen, and we've got to deal with it, Em, no matter how difficult it is. And that won't be easy. It's understandable if your subconscious is unsettled.'

Emma nodded, relieved that Dan understood. She decided to tell him everything on her mind. 'In the past day, I've also been thinking about Firework Films. About whether they're still planning to finish that television programme . . .'

Firework Films, a dirt-digging production company, known for its exploitative reality TV shows, was making a docudrama of what had happened to Emma and Dan over the past summer.

'I think we have to assume that they will.'

'It's just that as we haven't heard anything more from Adrian Spencer, I thought it might be a good sign.'

Adrian Spencer, a researcher for the company, had been pestering them incessantly for information, but after they had complained directly to the company, his unwanted attention had stopped.

'I wouldn't bet on it, unfortunately.'

'I know. But I really wish they wouldn't.'

'Me too. But we have no control over what they do, do we? All we can try and do is deal with it in the best way we can – try not to let it affect us too much. Though that's easier said than done, I know.'

'You're right,' Emma said, sitting up and taking a larger swig from her glass. 'We need to focus on the positives.'

'Yes. Like your new job.' Dan grinned at her.

Emma's new acting role in a West End play was, indeed, a really positive thing. Rehearsals weren't due to start for a few weeks, but she had received the script via her agent, and had already read it through several times. Each time, she had felt more and more excited by it.

Dan glanced up from his menu. 'And have you made a decision about the reunion?'

Emma had also received an invitation to attend a reunion event the following weekend for the cast of *Up My Street*, the soap opera in which she had spent five, largely happy, years. The event was to celebrate the twenty-year anniversary of the show and the move of the production to brand-new, state-of-the-art studios at Media City, a massive development at Salford Quays, not far from their aging base in central Manchester. She had made many wonderful friends during her time on the show, both in front of and behind the camera, so it would be amazing to see her old colleagues again.

'I'm still not sure.'

There were some things that made Emma hesitate in accepting the invitation: that time had been, in many ways, the breeding ground for everything bad that had happened since.

It was where she had met and fallen in love with Stuart Harris. And it was where she had first come to the attention of Stephen Myers – the desperate, needy stalker who had made the latter stages of her time on the show an absolute misery.

Emma looked out at the ocean. A huge container ship was moving across the distant horizon, possibly heading for one of the big African ports. Their tour guide that day had explained how much shipping traffic passed through, either stopping off at the island or gliding past its shores. She noticed too that the sky was darkening purple and black in the distance – the guide had also warned them that a big storm would roll in that evening.

'Looks like the storm's approaching,' Dan said, seeing where she was looking.

The thought made Emma shiver a little: thunder and lightning always unnerved her. One of her first memories of childhood was cowering under her bedcovers during a storm, wishing that the noise would stop. Her parents had come to the rescue, letting her sleep in their bed that night.

'It's up to you, of course, but I think you should go to the reunion,' Dan said. 'It might be a good way to move on.'

'But aren't reunions about looking back to the past?'

'Maybe to deal with the past, you've got to face the past.'

Emma smiled. 'Maybe you're right. You think it might help stop the dream?'

Dan shrugged. 'Who knows? I'm not a psychologist. But, at the very least, you should have a good time.'

'And what if Charlotte Harris is there?'

Charlotte Harris, Stuart's younger sister, had played a non-speaking part in the soap opera – Stuart had managed to get her the role of one of the children in the school that sometimes featured.

'She probably won't have got an invite. But if she is, then just try to ignore her.'

'I guess.' Emma certainly didn't relish the idea of seeing her again. Not after what Charlotte had said to her at their last meeting, two months ago – blaming Emma for Stuart's suicide and for the break-up of his relationship with Sally.

'Don't let Charlotte Harris stop you from going. If you really don't want to go, then fair enough, but if it's the thought of her being there that's putting you off, then that's different.'

'You're right. I will go.' Emma nodded briskly, smiling at him. 'And you're right about needing to face up to the past in order to move on. I'm thinking of maybe going to see a counsellor. Maybe the colleague of Miranda's that she recommended, the last time I was round with her and Dad. She said she'd see me on a more informal basis. What do you think?'

'I think you should do whatever you feel you need to do. I'll support you, whatever you decide.'

'And you? Do you think you might benefit from counselling?'

Dan smiled. 'I think I'll be okay.'

The storm hit just as they finished their meal. They ran back to their room as the rain began to fall heavily and, within minutes, water was cascading down the guttering and pooling across the balcony. Emma and Dan watched from the comfort of their room as the sky flashed and thunder boomed.

The intense, powerful storm raged on throughout the night, and Emma didn't sleep very well. But at least the dream didn't return. And, by morning, all was calm.